TREASURES OF THE SNOW

TREASURES OF THE SNOW

A STORY OF SWITZERLAND

by Patricia M. St. John

SCRIPTURE UNION
5 Wigmore Street, London W1H 0AD

First published 1950
Reprinted 1951
Reprinted 1952
Reprinted 1954
Reprinted 1955
Reprinted 1957
Reprinted 1961
Reprinted 1967
First published in paperback edition 1964
Reprinted 1969
Reprinted in this form 1971

ISBN 0 85421 153 5

By the same author

THE TANGLEWOOD'S SECRET

STAR OF LIGHT

THREE GO SEARCHING

Printed in the Republic of Ireland
by Cahill and Company Limited,
Parkgate Printing Works, Dublin

Chapter One

It was Christmas Eve, and Dani was five years old. It was a great day, because for the first time in his life he had been considered old enough to go down to the church with Annette and to see the tree.

Now he sat up in bed, drinking a bowl of potato soup, his yellow head only just showing above his enormous white feather eiderdown which was almost as fat as it was broad. Annette sat beside him, and in her hand she held a shining gingerbread bear.

"I am sorry, Dani," she announced firmly, "but you cannot have it in bed with you. It would be all crumbs by the morning. Look! I will put him here on the cupboard and the moon will shine in on him so that you can see him."

Dani opened his mouth to argue, but changed his mind, and filled his mouth with potato soup. It was unreasonable of his sister to object to his hugging his bear all night, but, after all, there were lots of other things to be happy about. Dani was always happy from the moment when he opened his eyes in the morning to the moment he closed them at night. Tonight he was specially happy because he had heard the bells and seen the glittering tree, and been out in the snow by starlight. He handed his empty bowl to Annette and cuddled down under his feather-bed duvet.

"Do you think," he asked confidently, "that Father Christmas would come if I put my slippers on the windowsill?" Annette looked rather startled, and wondered where he had heard of such a thing, for in Switzerland Father Christmas is not such a well-known person as he is in England. Swiss children have their Christmas bear from the tree on Christmas Eve, and presents from their family on New Year's Day. On Christmas Day they go to church and have a feast, but few children get a present.

"They said," went on Dani, "that he came on a sleigh drawn by reindeer, and left presents in good children's slippers. Am I a good child, Annette?"

"Yes," answered Annette, kissing him, "you are a very good child, but you will not get a present from Father Christmas. He only goes to rich little boys."

"Aren't I a rich little boy?" asked Dani, who thought life left nothing to be desired.

"No," replied Annette firmly, "you are not. We are poor and Papa has to work hard, and Grandmother and I have to go on and on patching your clothes because we cannot afford to buy new ones."

Dani chuckled. "I don't mind being poor," he announced stoutly; "I like it. Now tell me a story, Annette; tell me about Christmas and the little Baby and the cows and the great big shining star."

So Annette told the story, and Dani, who should have been asleep, listened wide-eyed.

"I should have liked sleeping in the hay better than in the inn," he said when she had finished. "I should like to sleep with Paquerette; I think it would be fun."

Annette shook her head. "No, you wouldn't," she replied; "not in the winter, without a duvet; you would be very cold and unhappy and long for a warm bed. It was cruel of them to say there was no room for a little new baby; they could have made room somehow."

The cuckoo clock on the stairs struck nine. Annette jumped up.

"You must go to sleep, Dani," she said, "and I must make Papa's chocolate."

She kissed him, tucked him up, put out the light and left him; but Dani did not go to sleep. Instead, he lay staring out into the darkness, thinking hard.

He was not a greedy little boy, but he could not help thinking that if Father Christmas happened to come to their house it would be a great pity not to be ready. Of course, it was unlikely he would come, since Dani was only a poor child, but on the other hand it was just possible that he might. And, after all, it could do no harm to put out the little slipper even if there were nothing in it in the morning. He could put it just outside the back door on the little strip of snow that divided the kitchen from the hay barn. Of course, Father Christmas was very unlikely to see it there, but still, there was no harm in trying.

Dani's mind was made up. He crept out of bed and tiptoed cautiously across the bedroom and down the stairs. He went barefoot, because he did not want anyone to hear him, and in his hand he carried one small scarlet slipper, lined with rabbit fur. His father had shot the rabbit, and Annette had made the slippers, and Dani felt it might catch the eye of Father Christmas. It was a struggle to lift the great wooden bar that latched the kitchen door, and Dani had to stand on a stool before he managed it. He had a moment's bright vision of snow and starlight, and then the bitter air struck him like a knife, and almost took his breath away. He thrust the slipper on to the step, and shut the door again as quickly as he could.

Back to bed scuttled Dani with a light heart. He cuddled down under the clothes, curled himself into a ball, and buried his nose in the pillows. He had already said his proper prayers with Annette before he got into bed, and now he had a little bit to add.

"Please, dear God," he whispered, "make Father Christmas and his reindeer come this way; and make him see my red slipper, and make him put a little present inside even if I am only a poor boy."

And then the hump that was Dani rolled over sideways, and fell asleep to dream, like thousands of other children the world over, of the old Gentleman in the red cloak careering over the snow to the jangle of reindeer bells.

He woke very early, and of course the first thing he thought of was the scarlet slipper. It was such an exciting thought that his heart beat quite thumpily, and he peeped over the top of his duvet to see whether Annette was awake.

But Annette was fast asleep, with her long fair hair spread all over the pillow, and for all Dani knew it might still have been the middle of the night. In fact, he had almost decided that it must still be the middle of the night when he heard his father clattering the milk churns in the kitchen below.

So it must be Christmas morning, and he must get down quickly or his father would open the door and find his present before he did; for somehow Dani was absolutely sure that there would be a present.

He crept out of the room without waking Annette, and slipped into the kitchen where his father was scalding the churns. His father did not see him until he felt two arms clasping his legs, and looked down; there was his son, rosy, bright-eyed and tousled, looking up at him.

"Has Father Christmas been?" asked Dani. Surely his father, who stayed up so late, and got up so early, must have heard the bells and the crunch of hoofs in the snow.

"Father Christmas?" repeated his father in bewilderment. "Why, no; he didn't come here. We live too far up the mountain for him."

But Dani shook his head. "We don't," he said eagerly. "His reindeers can go anywhere, and I expect you were asleep and didn't hear him. Open the door for me, Papa dear, just in case he has left me a present."

His father wished he had known of this earlier, so that he could have put a chocolate stick on the step, for he hated to disappoint his boy. However, open the back door he must, to roll the churns across to the stable; so he lifted the latch, and in an instant Dani had dived between his legs like an eager rabbit, and was kneeling by his slipper in the snow.

Then he gave a wild, high-pitched scream of excitement and dived back again into the kitchen with his slipper in his arms.

A miracle had happened: Father Christmas had been and had left a present, and in all his happy five years of life Dani had never had such a perfect present before.

For curled up in the furry lining of his scarlet slipper was a tiny white kitten, with blue eyes and one black smudge on her nose. It was a weak, thin little kitten, very nearly dead with cold and hunger, and had it not been for the warmth of the rabbit's fur it would certainly have been quite dead. But it still breathed lightly, and Dani's father, forgetting all about the churns, knelt down on the kitchen floor beside his son and set about restoring it.

First he wrapped it in a piece of hot flannel and laid it against the hot wall of the stove; then they heated milk in a pan and fed it with a spoon, as it was far too weak to suck. At first it only spluttered and dribbled, but after a while it put out a wee pink tongue and its dim blue eyes grew bright and interested. Then, after about five minutes or so, it twitched its tail and stretched itself. Finally, having had quite enough to eat, it curled itself back into a ball and set up a faint, contented purr.

All this time Dani and his father had not spoken one word, because they were so intent on what they were doing. But, now that their work was successfully finished for the time being, they sat back and looked at each other. Dani's cheeks were the colour of poppies and his eyes shone like stars.

"I knew he would come," he whispered, "but I never guessed he would bring such a beautiful present; it is the most beautiful present I have ever had in all my life. What shall I call it, Papa?"

"You had better call it Klaus after the Christmas saint," said Papa; and he looked curiously at Dani with a sort of new respect. It certainly seemed like a miracle.

He left the sleeping kitten in Dani's care and went to the stables. Sitting in the dim light with his head pressed against the flanks of the cows and the milk frothing into the pails he tried to think of some explanation. Of course the kitten had strayed across from the barn, but it did seem wonderful that it should have found Dani's slipper and been there all ready for him. After a while Dani's father decided that perhaps it was not so wonderful after all. Surely it was natural on Christmas night that the Father in Heaven, thinking of His own Son, should have been unwilling to disappoint a motherless child on earth. Surely He had guided the steps of the white kitten for the sake of the Babe born in Bethlehem. Dani's father paused for a moment in his milking and thanked God on behalf of his little son.

Annette appeared in the kitchen shortly afterwards to get breakfast, and stood still in amazement at the sight of Dani in his night-shirt and overcoat watching over a white kitten. She was about to ask questions when Dani put his finger on his lips and motioned her to be quiet, for he was very much afraid of waking the kitten. Then he tiptoed over to her, pulled her down on a chair, climbed on to her knee and whispered the whole strange story into her ear.

Annette had no difficulty in explaining it to herself. Being eleven years old she did not believe in Father Christmas, but she did believe in Christmas angels, and surely such a pure white kitten must have dropped straight from heaven. She sat down on the floor and gathered Dani and the kitten on to her lap; and here Grandmother found them half an hour later when she came in expecting to find her Christmas coffee steaming on the table.

Chapter Two

LUCIEN lay under his large feather-bed eiderdown and wished it was not time to get up. His bed was so warm, and the nipped air outside so cold. He sighed and cuddled down again under the clothes.

"Lucien!" His mother's voice sounded really angry, and Lucien jumped up in a hurry. This was the third time she had called him, and before, he had pretended not to hear. He could still get up and be in time for school, although he would not have time to do the milking. But, after all, if he didn't do the milking his mother would have to, and these days she did it more often than not.

"Other boys don't have to milk before they go to school," muttered Lucien as he buttoned his jacket, "and I don't see why I should always have to work harder than everyone else just because I don't happen to have a father."

He went downstairs looking sulky and defiant, and sat down to gobble up his bread and coffee. His mother came in from the stable when he was half-way through.

"Lucien!" she said sharply, "why don't you get up when I call you? It happens day after day! You're no help to me in the mornings at all. Your sister gets up early enough and goes off to work without any fuss. I know other boys have fathers, but we've only three cows and we can't live without them. You're a big, strong boy now, and it's shameful that you should leave all the early work to me like this."

Lucien scowled. "I work at night," he whined; "I

never get any play. I have to fetch in the wood, and I have to come farther up the hill than any of the others, and I fetch down the fodder for you, and clean the shed on Saturdays."

His mother sniffed. "I've usually done most of it by the time you get home from school," she retorted. "I know you don't get as much time in the winter as other children, but I do all I can, and this early-morning milking is wearing me out. You're quite old enough to undertake it, and in future you're to get up properly. Now hurry off or you'll be late for school."

Lucien struggled into his cloak, and turned away with a sulky good-bye. He unhitched his sledge and went whizzing away into the frosty dark. Save for the smooth sound of his own runners the world was quite silent with that tremendous silence that holds its breath before the coming of dawn. The enormousness of it usually awed Lucien a little, but to-day he was too cross to think about it.

"It's jolly unfair!" he muttered. "Everyone's against me—it's not my fault I don't get my lessons done properly; I'm always having to work at home. It's mark-reading to-day, and I suppose I shall be bottom again, and that swanky Annette Burnier top. I bet she doesn't have to milk the cows before school. . . . OH! . . .! !"

He tried to stop, but it was too late; he had reached the fork in the path, and he had been so busy feeling cross that he had not looked where he was going. He had bumped straight into Annette's sledge sideways, and lifted her clean into the ditch.

It was a careless bit of work, and Lucien, crimson in the face and truly distressed, jumped off his sledge to help, but Annette was before him. She had never liked Lucien much, and she was badly shaken. She turned on him, waist deep in snow, her eyes blazing.

"You great clumsy donkey!" she shouted, half crying.

"Can't you look where you are going? Look at my copy-book—all my exercise is smudged and torn! I shall tell the master it's all your fault."

Lucien, who was never good at keeping his temper, lost it at once.

"All right!" he shouted back, "there's no need to make such a fuss; I didn't do it on purpose. Anyone would think I'd killed you instead of tearing your old exercise-book. It won't hurt you to lose your marks. I'm going on."

He jumped on to his sledge and whizzed away, arriving just in time for school.

"She's only got to get out," he muttered, "and I don't suppose she would have let me help her in any case. Thank goodness I'm in time for school; I've been late twice this week already."

But getting out of that snowdrift was a very different matter from getting in, and poor Annette had quite a struggle. By the time she had extricated herself and collected her books, she was crying in real earnest—crying with cold and shock, and sore knees and, most of all, crying with rage. And when she crept into school a quarter of an hour later, her eyes were red and her nose was blue and her poor raw hands and knees were grazed and bleeding—what with her wet exercise-book and her torn reader she certainly looked a sorry sight.

"Annette," said the master, quite concerned, "what has happened to you, my child?"

For a few seconds Annette fought hard with the temptation to tell tales, but the sight of Lucien sitting so smug and safe in his desk was too much for her.

"It was Lucien," she burst out angrily; "he knocked me into a ditch, and went off and left me. I couldn't get out." She stuffed her knuckles into her eyes and began crying again. She was really very badly shaken, and oh, so angry!

The school drew in its breath with righteous indignation, and the wretched Lucien hung his head, and looked very sullen indeed.

The master caned Lucien for behaving in such an ungentlemanly way, whereupon, sad to relate, Annette cheered up and felt better. Then later the marks were read out, and Annette came out top and felt better still; Lucien came out bottom and was told to stay in and do extra work after school. So he sat through morning school, and lunched with the others, and came back to afternoon school, and sat on alone when the others had gone, and all the time the rage and hatred and ill-temper in his heart were getting bigger and bigger till he felt as if he were going to burst.

At last he was free, and wandering up the hill dragging his sledge behind him. What a terrible day it had been! His mother had been cross with him, Annette had told tales about him, the master had caned him, and he had come bottom.

The shadows on the fields were strangely blue that night—a sort of unearthly blue, like the blue of mists in far valleys, and high up, the mountain-tops were still sunlit, with ragged wisps of cloud trailing about them. As he trudged up the hill, Lucien's rage began to give place to a sort of weary misery, and, thinking he was alone, he too began to cry a little.

And then he suddenly discovered that he was not alone. He was again at the place where the path divided, and a little boy was standing in the snow looking up at him in great astonishment—a happy, rosy-cheeked, bright-eyed little boy, his fair hair sticking out like a thatch from under his woolly cap, his face glowing with good health and good humour.

It was Dani, making a snowman; he had just put on the head, and was arranging the eyes. It was the best snowman Dani had ever made, and he was just about to fetch Annette to look at it.

"Why are you crying?" asked Dani, tactlessly.

"I'm not crying!" retorted Lucien, angrily.

"Ooh, you are!" replied Dani, "and I know why . . . it's because the master caned you; Annette told us."

He did not mean to be cruel, for he was usually a kind little boy. But Lucien had been nasty to Annette and that, to Dani, was quite unpardonable. Lucien's temper flared up instantly, and lifting his foot he kicked Dani's snowman into little bits. Dani lifted up his voice and gave a loud howl of alarm and disappointment.

Annette, crossing from the shed, saw what was happening in an instant. She flew down the path like a young tigress, and slapped Lucien full in the face. Lucien lifted his hand to retaliate, but the sight of Monsieur Burnier coming out of the chalet with a bucket made him think better of it; everything was clearly against him.

"Sneak—tell-tale—coward!" shouted Lucien. "Baby! coming into school crying like that."

"Great rough bully," shouted back Annette, "leaving me in the ditch like that, and then kicking poor Dani's snowman. He never did you any harm; why can't you leave him alone? I'm jolly glad you were caned! Come on, Dani, come home."

She marched angrily off up the path, with Dani trotting behind her, but at the door of the chalet she turned and noticed a patch of pink sky behind the far mountains. Once Grandmother had taught her a text from the Bible which said, "Let not the sun go down upon your wrath" —she suddenly thought of it now. Well, there was still time—Lucien was still there. After all it was nasty of her to have told tales. She hesitated.

But no—he'd been much worse than she had; it was for him to say he was sorry. If she asked him to forgive her it would sound as if she were to blame, and of course she wasn't—oh, no, not in the least! She went in and slammed the door behind her.

Lucien went slowly home with his face stinging from that slap, more furious than he had been all day long. But, as he walked, he glanced up and noticed a wonderful thing. The clouds had come up in a purple bank, blotting out the mountain behind his home; but just in one spot they had broken, and in that rift Lucien could see the snowy crest, radiant with golden light. Used as he was to winter sunsets, the beauty of this made Lucien catch his breath and look again. And the pure, high radiance suddenly made his anger seem a small, poor thing, not worth hanging on to. How nice it would be to start again! There was still time to catch Annette if he ran.

But no! Annette was a swank, and would probably take no notice of him, and, anyhow, why should he apologize to a girl?

So, because neither would be the first to forgive, the quarrel began—a quarrel that was to last many a long day and was to bring in its train a great deal of unhappiness for them both.

Chapter Three

ANNETTE's birthday took place in March, and Dani thought about it for weeks beforehand, for nothing pleased Dani so much as giving presents. And this time, besides his presents, he had planned a big surprise. His curly head was full of it, and as soon as Annette had gone to school Dani explained his plan to Grandmother. She was sitting on the verandah in the spring sunshine chopping dandelion leaves for that evening's soup when her little grandson came up and rested his elbows on her knee.

"Grandmother," announced Dani. "I'm going up the mountain to where the snow has melted, to pick soldanellas and crocuses for Annette's birthday. I will put them on the breakfast table with all my presents."

His grandmother, who hated his being out of her sight, looked doubtful.

"You are too little to go up the mountain alone," she replied. "The slopes are slippery and you will fall into the snowdrifts."

"Klaus will go with me," said Dani earnestly.

Grandmother chuckled. "A lot of good may she do you," she retorted.

Dani picked his kitten up round the middle, kissed Grandmother, and stumped off down the balcony steps, singing. Crash! crash! went his hobnailed boots, and his voice rose loud and clear. His grandmother strained her dim old eyes to watch him until out of sight, then she gave a little sigh and went on with her dandelions. He was growing so big and independent, and in a very short time he must start at the Infant School. He was a baby no longer.

Dani trotted on up the slopes, and Klaus picked her way delicately behind him, for although she was a Christmas kitten she hated walking in the snow. It was a beautiful day, and spring was clothing the mountains and melting the drifts. Already the fields were green beside the river in the valley, and the cows were grazing out of doors. Up here on the higher slopes the snow was beginning to yield, and patches of pale yellow grass were strewed amongst them, while the streams were swollen to overflowing with clear green ice-water.

Klaus continued to pick her way until she reached the low stone wall at the edge of the field. On the other side of this stone wall was a rocky ravine with a rushing torrent at the bottom. In summer the rocks were like fairy gardens, with harebells and saxifrage and cushions of pink soapwort growing all over them, but now they were bare and brown. Klaus sat on the wall and fluffed out her fur in the spring sunshine. Then she started to wash herself all over, which was unnecessary because she was already almost as white as the snow.

Dani wandered from yellow patch to yellow patch gathering flowers. The field was gay with pale mauve crocuses and bright primulas that followed the windings of the streams in the grass like little pink paths. Dani loved them, but what he loved best of all were the soldanellas. They could not even wait for the snow to melt, but pushed right up through the frozen edges of the drifts, their frail stems encased in ice. Their flowers, like fringed mauve bells, hung downwards.

Dani was so happy. The sun shone on him and the flowers smiled up at him, and he told himself stories about tiny goblins who lived in caves under the snow; their beards were white and their caps were red and they were full of mischief. Sometimes if there was no one looking they came out and swung on the soldanella bells—Annette had said so.

For this reason he approached each fresh soldanella clump on tiptoe, and kept his eyes fixed on their bowed heads. And that was why he never heard footsteps approaching until they were quite close, and then he looked up suddenly with a little start.

Lucien stood close behind him, with a rather unpleasant look on his face, and a queer gleam of triumph in his eyes; for Lucien had not forgotten the blow that Annette had given him when Dani had screamed for help. Ever since that day he had planned some revenge, and when he had seen Dani's little figure standing alone in the high pasture he had hurried to the spot. Of course he would not hurt such a tiny child, but it would be fun to tease and annoy him, and pay him back for telling tales. At least he could take his flowers from him.

"Who are you picking those for?" demanded Lucien.

"For Annette," replied Dani stoutly. He had a feeling that Lucien would not like this answer, but Annette had told him that he must always speak the truth, even when he was frightened.

Lucien gave a horrid laugh.

"I hate Annette," he announced. "She is a proud, stuck-up swank. But at school she is a dunce; the little ones in the Infant School are better at arithmetic than she is. She knows no more than her own cows. Give those flowers to me; she shall not have them!"

Dani was so shocked at this speech that he went bright pink, and put his flowers behind his back. How could anyone hate Annette?—Annette who was so beautiful and so good, and so clever and so wise.

"You can't have them," said Dani, holding the bunch tightly in his small hands. "They are mine."

"I shall take them," replied Lucien. "You are only a baby and you can't fight against me. I shall do as I please to you. You are a little tell-tale and I shall pay you out."

He snatched the bunch roughly from Dani's grasp and flung them on the ground and trampled on them; Dani stared for a moment at the crushed soldanellas and bruised crocuses, and then burst into a loud howl. He had spent the whole happy afternoon gathering those flowers, and now they were all wasted. Then he flung himself on Lucien and began beating him with his small fists.

"I shall tell my daddy," he shouted. "I shall go straight home and tell him this very minute and he will come to your house and he will beat you. You are a cruel, wicked boy."

Now this was exactly what Lucien did not wish to happen, for, like most bullies, he was cowardly, and was afraid of Dani's father. Dani's father was as tall and strong as a giant, and any ill-treatment of his son would certainly rouse him to fury. Lucien held Dani firmly by the wrists to stop him punching, and looked round the field, considering what he could do to frighten the little boy into silence.

His gaze suddenly fell on Klaus sunning herself on the wall, and an idea struck him. He pushed Dani away and walked rapidly towards the ravine, and Dani, who thought his tormentor had left him, wiped away the tears with the back of his hand and began picking fresh flowers as fast as he could. Lucien or no Lucien, Annette's birthday table must be gay and beautiful.

Suddenly Lucien's voice came ringing across the field; Dani looked up quickly, and what he saw made him feel quite sick for a moment. Lucien was standing by the wall holding Klaus out at arm's length by the scruff of her neck—holding her right over the dark ravine and the rushing torrent of melted ice.

"Unless you come here at once, and promise not to tell tales to your father," called Lucien, "I shall drop your kitten into the stream."

Dani began to run, stumbling blindly over the snow-drifts, but his legs were trembling and he could not run fast. The thought of Klaus carried away helpless in that swirling brown current filled him with such horror that his mouth went dry and he could not cry out. He only knew that he must get there and snatch his kitten out of the grasp of that wicked boy and never, never let it go again.

Now let it be said here, right at the beginning of the story, that Lucien never for one moment meant to drop Klaus. He was unkind, and a bully, but he was not a murderer. But Klaus was not used to being held by the scruff of the neck, and after a moment or two she began to struggle. Finding that she was not released she struggled more violently, and then finally, getting frantic, she did what she had never done before. She put up her front paw and gave Lucien a sharp scratch.

And Lucien, who was watching Dani's stumbling progress, was taken by surprise and let go. Klaus dropped like a stone into the ravine, just as Dani, white and tearful, reached the wall.

Dani did not hesitate a single moment. He gave a shriek like some small terrified animal caught in a trap, and hurled himself over the low wall, before Lucien, quite paralysed for a few seconds by what he had done, had time to grab hold of him and pull him back.

After that everything happened in a few seconds. Klaus had not fallen into the water. She had stuck fast on a ledge of overhanging rock and clung there mewing piteously. An older child might have reached her safely and scrambled back, but Dani was only five. The face of the rock was wet and Dani's feet slipped just as he reached his kitten. He gave another scream—a scream that haunted Lucien for years to come—and disappeared over the edge.

Had Lucien not been half stupid with panic he would have scrambled down after him and peered over into the ravine. But it never occurred to him that Dani could be anything but dead, and to see the body of the child carried away by the current, down towards the waterfall, was more than he could bear. He sank down on the grass in a limp little heap and covered his face with his arm; and, had Annette seen him at that moment, even she might have realized that Lucien had certainly been punished.

"Dani is drowned," he moaned over and over again. "I have killed him. What shall I do? Oh, what shall I do?"

But gradually a cowardly idea came into his mind, and he sprang up and looked round wildly. Time was getting on. They would soon come and look for Dani, and then they would find him and everyone would know that he was a murderer. No one so far knew that he had had anything to do with the accident, and, if he hurried home and behaved as if nothing had happened, no one ever would know. He must escape.

He ran like a hunted rabbit into the shelter of the pine-wood, with his heart beating furiously and his head throbbing. He dared not go home just yet, but he made his way round by lonely paths, so that if anyone should see him coming it would look as though he had come in another direction. Every few minutes he thought he heard footsteps following and leaped round to look. But there was no one there.

At last he reached his own back door, and here he stopped. No, he could not go in. He could not face his mother, who believed in him, with that dreadful black secret in his heart. Surely she would see it in his face. He could not look the same as before. He was a murderer.

Perhaps later he would summon up courage to face her, but not yet, for his teeth were chattering so, and she would ask what was the matter. In the meantime he must hide. He looked round wildly for some place, and saw the ladder leaning against the barn where the straw was stored in the attic above the cowshed. Up the ladder went Lucien, and then flinging himself face downward in the chaff he sobbed as though his heart would break.

Chapter Four

THE old grandmother finished shredding the dandelions and then, leaning heavily on her stick, went back into the house and sat down in her chair; she was very, very tired, and soon her head nodded on her breast and she fell asleep.

Grandmother slept much longer than usual. Annette had gone down to the village to shop, and Father was up in the forest cutting and stacking logs. She had meant to turn the heel of Dani's white woollen stockings, and put patches on the elbows of his blue linen overalls, but she was much too tired. She just folded her knotted old hands on her lap and went on sleeping; and the cuckoo jumped out of the clock and struck three without waking her.

It was nearly four when Grandmother woke and looked at the clock, and then she gave a little exclamation of anxiety and surprise. Dani had gone out at half-past two and had not yet returned. Where could he be?

"Dani!" she called out sharply, for he might be hiding. Perhaps in a moment he would tumble out of the cupboard, mischievous and gleeful.

But there was no answer, and Grandmother hobbled on to the verandah and shaded her dim eyes. Perhaps she would catch sight of him stumping home, and how she would scold him for being so late!

A figure appeared round the cow-shed, but it was not Dani. It was Annette with her basket on her back and a long golden loaf sticking out of the top of it. She had had a half-holiday and had been shopping. She waved to Grandmother and came running up the steps.

"Annette," said Grandmother, "take your basket off and go and search for your little brother. He went out to pick flowers nearly an hour and a half ago and he hasn't come back."

Annette let down her basket with a bump. She privately thought that her grandmother was rather fussy about Dani. What harm could come to him, wandering about in fields where anyone he might meet knew him and loved him?

"He will be up in the woods with Papa," she replied. "I'll go up and see in a few minutes. Let me have a piece of bread and jam first, Grandma. I'm hungry."

She broke off a thick hunk from the loaf, and spread it with butter and jam, while her grandmother went back to the balcony and peered up the path again. Then while she was eating, firm footsteps were heard down the hill-side and Father came into sight.

"Where is Dani?" cried Grandmother. "Has he not been with you, Pierre? Did you not meet him up the mountain?"

"Dani?" repeated Father in astonishment. "He has not been near me. When did he leave you, Mother?"

Grandmother gave up trying to hide her anxiety and wrung her hands. "He left me over an hour and a half ago," she cried. "He and the kitten. They went out to pick crocuses in the field nearby. Something must have happened to him!"

Annette and her father looked at each other, and both were worried, for the path from the forest led through the crocus fields and Father had seen no sign of Dani when on the way home. Annette slipped her hand into her father's.

"Perhaps he has wandered into the forest to look for you," she said reassuringly. "Let's go and look for him.

Klaus will probably be about somewhere to show us which direction he's gone in. Klaus hates long walks."

Together they set out up the hill towards the forest, but they went in silence, for the father was afraid to voice his thoughts. The spring brings certain dangers to mountains in Switzerland—swollen torrents and sudden falls of melting snow called avalanches, and Dani was such a tiny boy.

Grandmother, left alone, went indoors and prayed, and as she prayed she saw a picture, for the less Grandmother saw with her outward eyes the more she saw with her mind. And this time there seemed to rise before her the picture of a dark forest, furrowed by deep rushing streams, its paths rough with boulders and blocked with avalanches. Along this path ran Dani with his hands full of crocuses, and beside him walked an angel with white wings, and in the shadow of those wings there was shelter and warmth and safety.

"In Heaven their angels do always behold the face of My Father which is in Heaven," whispered Grandmother, and she rose from her knees feeling quite peaceful, and began to prepare the evening meal.

There was still no sign of Dani or Klaus in the fields, nor at the edge of the pinewoods. Up and down they searched calling his name, but nothing answered except the echoes and the rushing of the torrent, and gradually the sun sank towards the peaks and the shadows grew longer on the fields.

"Papa," said Annette suddenly, "I wonder if he has gone down to Lucien's house. I have seen Lucien talking to him once or twice. I will run down to their chalet and ask."

Over the drifts and the grass she bounded and reached Madame Morel's chalet in less than five minutes. The back door stood open, and Annette put her head round.

"Madame," she called, "Lucien! Are you there? Have you seen Dani?"

The house was silent and deserted, yet they could not have gone far for they had left the door wide open. Annette was about to run across to the barns when she caught sight of Madame Morel's stout figure toiling up the track that led to their own chalet. Annette ran to meet her.

"Madame," she cried eagerly, catching hold of her hand, "have you seen our little Dani? He has run away, and we have not seen him for two hours. Do you think he might be with Lucien, and, if so, where is Lucien?"

"He may well be," answered Madame Morel rather grimly; "I have just been down to your chalet to ask if you could give me any news of Lucien. The lazy boy should have been home long ago, and the cow is crying out to be milked. I shall have to do her myself, unless he has arrived while I was away. If so, he will have gone straight to the shed. Let us go across and see."

They went together over to the barn and opened the heavy wooden door. The red cow was stamping and twitching her tail, but there was no Lucien to be seen. Madame turned away with an exclamation of annoyance and was just about to close the door, when Annette seized hold of her sleeve and held up her finger.

"Listen!" she whispered; "what is that noise up in the loft?"

They both stood listening intently for a moment. From the straw dump above came the unmistakable sound of a child's stifled sobs.

Annette was up the ladder in an instant and Madame Morel lumbered up behind her. Both knew that something was desperately wrong, but Annette thought only of Dani and Madame thought only of Lucien.

"Lucien!" cried Madame, "my poor child, what is the matter? Are you hurt?"

"Dani," hissed Annette, seizing him by the arm and shaking him, "where is he? What have you done with him? Give him back!"

Lucien cowered lower in the straw, and shook his head violently. He was quite hysterical by now.

"I don't . . . know . . . where . . . he . . . is," he screamed. "It wasn't my fault."

"*What* wasn't your fault?" Annette screamed back, shaking him worse than ever. "Where is he? You do know—you are telling lies! Madame, make him speak the truth!"

Madame dragged Annette out of the way and knelt down by Lucien. Her face was very white, for by now she had guessed that some harm had come to Dani and that Lucien knew of it. She pulled his face up from the straw, and turned it towards her.

"Lucien," she commanded, trying to speak quietly, "speak at once. Where is Dani?"

Lucien stared at her wildly and saw that escape was impossible.

"He's dead," he said with a hiccough, and began to cry again with his head buried in the straw.

Annette had heard, but she did not move, for just for a few moments she had lost all power of movement. Her face was so ashen in the dim light that Madame thought she was going to faint, and tried to put her arms round her, but Annette sprang away. Then she spoke in a hoarse voice that did not sound like her own any longer.

"He must come and show us where," she said at last. "And at least my father can carry him home. And later," she added, as an afterthought, "I will kill Lucien."

Madame took no notice of the last part of this speech,

but the first suggestion sounded sensible. She took her boy by the arm, dragged him to his feet and almost carried him down the ladder.

"Come, Lucien," she urged at the bottom, "you must show us where Dani is, quickly—otherwise Monsieur Burnier will be here with the police to make you go."

This threat frightened a little bit of sense and reason into Lucien, and he set off up the hill as fast as he could go, sobbing all the time and protesting that it was not his fault. And Madame Morel and Annette followed. Madame Morel was sobbing as well, but Annette could not shed one tear; she felt as though all her tears were frozen up by rage and misery.

They reached the wall very quickly and Lucien pointed over into the darkening ravine. "He is over there, drowned in the torrent," he whispered, and then flung himself down and buried his face in the grass. At this moment, Monsieur Burnier appeared at the edge of the wood and hurried towards the little group.

He took no notice of Lucien, but took one look at his daughter and one look at the rocks, and in that quick glance he saw something that none of the others had noticed—a shivering white kitten crouching on a ledge, right on the crest of the overhanging boulder. Once he had seen this, no more words were needed for the moment. He simply said, "I must fetch a rope," and ran down the mountain like a man pursued by wild beasts.

Grandmother was at the door of the chalet, and she too saw written in his face all that she needed to know at that moment. Without a word, she watched him pull down his climbing rope that hung on the wall and bound away into the shadows.

"In the ravine," he suddenly called back; and then he disappeared.

Grandmother, left alone, put on a kettle, fetched out old linen and filled a large stone hot-water bottle, so as to be ready for anything. Then she sat down and shut her eyes and folded her hands. Once again she saw a picture of Dani, caught by the dark waters of the ravine; but the white wings of the angel stemmed the current and Dani was caught up safely into his arms.

"He shall give His angels charge over thee," whispered Grandmother, and she climbed the stairs to turn down his little bed and warm the blankets.

Dani's father was back with the rope in an amazingly short time, but to the watchers by the wall it seemed like hours. Nobody spoke as he secured it round a tree trunk and flung it over the boulder. Then gripping it with his hands and knees he ran down the slippery rocks and disappeared into the ravine. There, hanging in space, he dared to look down towards the rushing waters that must surely have carried away his child. And what he saw sent a great rush of hope into his heart, and a cry to his lips.

For Grandmother had seen right. The angels had taken charge of Dani as he fell, and he had never reached the water at all. He had fallen on to a jutting-out boulder just below, and there he lay, flat on his back, with his leg doubled up under him, waiting for someone to come and rescue him, and crying because he could not move. The time had been long and Dani supposed he had been to sleep, for he could never remember much about those two hours afterwards. He really remembered only the moment when his father hovered over him like some big bird, and then alighted by him and knelt on the rock at his side.

"Papa," whispered Dani, a little faintly, "where is Klaus?"

"Just above you," replied his father, devouring the little white face with his eyes. "We will pick her up on the way back."

"Papa," went on Dani, "my leg hurts and I can't move. Will you carry me home?"

"Of course," replied his father, "that is what I've come for. I'll carry you home at once." And he took his little son in his arms.

"But Papa," went on the anxious, feeble voice, "can you carry us both, Klaus and me together? You won't leave Klaus, will you? Because it is time she had her milk and she will be very thirsty."

"Klaus shall go in my pocket," promised his father, and he lifted the child very, very gently. Dani moaned, for his leg hurt dreadfully when moved. But he kept his eyes on his father's face and was really as brave as it is possible to be at five years old.

It was a long, slow journey back. Dani's father could not climb the rope with Dani in his arms; he had to scramble down to the edge of the torrent and pick his way along the side of it until they came to a part where the bank was less steep and he was able to make his way up. Dani mercifully sank into a sort of stupor, and seemed to know nothing until his father laid him down on the grass beside Annette.

"Have you got Klaus in your pocket?" said Dani, opening his eyes suddenly.

"I'm fetching her now," replied his father and, holding on to the rope, slid to the edge of the precipice again and picked up the white kitten. Dani held out his arms and Klaus nestled down against his heart, purring like a little steam engine. And Annette, for the first time in all that nightmare evening, burst into tears.

They laid him on a coat and Madame Morel and Monsieur Burnier carried him slowly home down the mountain, while Annette came behind carrying Klaus. A sad little procession, and yet their hearts were full of grateful joy, because Dani was alive, and had spoken. That for the moment was enough.

And no one, not even his mother, gave one thought to Lucien, who still lay under the wall, huddled down in the grass. When he lifted his head and found that he had been left alone with the night, he felt as though the whole world had cast him out and forgotten him. He got up, slunk home through the shadows, and crept, shivering, to bed, as lonely and miserable a little boy as ever walked this earth.

Chapter Five

DANI lay in his little bed between hot blankets, fully aware of the fact that he was a tremendously important person, and that anything he chose to ask for would be fetched immediately. As this had never been the case before, Dani was making the most of it.

Father stood at the end of the bed watching him and telling him all the funny stories he liked best; Annette sat on one side of him with a chocolate stick in her hand; Klaus was curled up on his chest purring; and Grandmother sat the other side with a bowl of cherry jam, and every time he asked for it she gave him a spoonful! If his leg had not been aching so, Dani would have thought he was in Heaven, and even as it was the cherry jam more than made up for the ache.

"Papa," said Dani, for about the tenth time, "are you quite, quite certain Klaus isn't hurt?"

"Quite certain," answered his father. "She drank a whole dish of milk, and ran upstairs with her tail up. Only healthy kittens would behave like that."

"Papa," went on Dani, opening his mouth like a baby bird for another mouthful of cherry jam, "it was Lucien who threw Klaus over the wall. Papa, it was very cruel of Lucien, wasn't it?"

"Very," replied his father, "and he shall certainly be punished." But Monsieur Burnier was too happy to have his son alive to think very much about Lucien. It was

Annette, sitting quietly by with a chocolate stick in her hand, who thought most about Lucien.

"I shall not be in a hurry," thought Annette to herself, "but I shall never, never forgive him as long as I live. One day I shall do something terrible to him. I shall never forgive him, never."

"'Nette," said Dani, "I want my chocolate stick, and then I want to go to sleep. And you must stay with me, 'Nette, because my leg hurts."

"Yes, chéri," answered Annette, handing him the chocolate stick. "I'll stay with you till you go to sleep."

Papa and Grandma kissed him and withdrew. Annette drew his head against her arm.

"Sing to me," commanded Dani. "Sing, 'Oh! que ta main paternelle, Me bénisse à mon coucher!'." It was Dani's little evening prayer that his grandmother had taught him—a prayer asking the Father in Heaven to forgive sins, to shelter little children under His wings for the night. Annette had often sung it before, but tonight she didn't want to. She could not really sing about forgiving sins when her heart was so full of hatred to Lucien that she could think of nothing but revenge.

"Not that one," said Annette; "I'll sing you another one about the bridge of Avignon. You say that one to yourself, Dani."

Dani pouted. Tonight Annette ought to do whatever he wanted.

"I don't like the one about the bridge at Avignon," he whined. "I want 'Oh! que ta main paternelle'."

"Oh, all right," said Annette with a little sigh. "I'll sing it if you like." And she sang it rather sadly. The first verses go like this in French;

Oh! que ta main paternelle
Me bénisse à mon coucher!
Et que ce soit sous ton aile
Que je dorme, ô mon Berger.

Veuille effacer par ta grâce
Les pécés que j'ai commis
Et que ton Esprit me fasse
*Obéissant et soumis.**

The tune is slow and haunting, and by the time Annette had finished Dani was fast asleep, dribbling out his chocolate stick on to the pillow. She laid her head down beside him, and once again she wept, for she was very tired and the relief had been so great. But they were not only tears of joy; for we cannot be truly happy if we hate someone.

She got up with a sigh and went downstairs.

"The doctor should be here soon," said Grandmother, "and then we shall have to wake him, poor little man. Never mind; let him sleep while he can."

"Grandmother," said Annette, looking up suddenly after a little silence, "Lucien must be punished. What is to be done to him? I can think of nothing that would pay him out for what he did."

The grandmother did not answer for a time. Then she replied. "Have you ever thought, Annette, that when we do wrong it often brings its own punishment without anyone else interfering? Think of Lucien's fright when he saw Dani fall, think of his misery and remorse tonight, and

---

*Oh, may the Hand of my Father,
Bless me as I go to sleep,
And beneath Thy wings of shelter
May Thy little children keep.

Wilt Thou forgive by Thy grace, Lord,
All wrong things I've done to-day.
May Thy Holy Spirit make me
Kind and ready to obey.

think of his shame and fear of others finding out what he did . . . and then think whether perhaps he has not been punished enough, and whether we should not forgive him and help him to start again."

Annette did not take much notice of Grandmother's words, except for one sentence. "Think of his fear of others finding out what he did." That was a splendid idea. She would see to it that they found out. Wherever she went she would tell everybody. She would tell it in the village and tell it at school, until everyone would hate him for his wickedness.

Her thoughts were interruped by a hurried knock at the door and Lucien's big sister burst into the room. She had arrived home from the town across the mountain where she worked, just in time to meet the slow little procession coming down from the fields, and had sped down to the village Post Office to 'phone the doctor who lived five miles up the valley.

"Dr. Pilliard can't come," she panted. "He has gone to another village to a sick woman and he won't be home till midnight and the last train's gone. They say you must take Dani in the cart to the hospital tomorrow morning and he will see him there."

"Thank you, Marie," said Grandmother. "It was good of you to go for us." She turned back to the kitchen. But Marie lingered full of curiosity.

"Tell me, Annette," she said, lowering her voice, "how did the accident happen? Why was my mother so silent and troubled?"

"It happened up the mountain," replied Annette shortly. "Lucien threw Dani's kitten over the ravine, and Dani tried to rescue him. Lucien did not try to stop Dani at all. I shouldn't wonder if he pushed him. I think Dani has broken his leg. He lay on the rocks for hours and Lucien never told anybody."

Marie went quite pale with horror, for she had never been particularly fond of her young brother.

"He shall be severely punished," she said angrily; "I will see to it myself"—and then flounced out of the house. Annette smiled. To turn his own family against Lucien was just what Annette wanted. She felt her revenge had begun.

There was nothing more to wait for now, so after a rather silent meal Annette dragged her way up to bed, tired and heavy-hearted. She lit a candle and stood looking at Dani through eyes that were misty with tears. He lay with his damp hair pushed back from his forehead and his arms flung out, and his usual peaceful look had gone. He was frowning even in his sleep, and now and then he moved his head restlessly and muttered troubled words.

Annette got into her bed by the window, but tired as she was she could not sleep. She felt strangely alone; then to her joy she heard slow, painful steps climbing the stairs and Grandmother came into the room—Grandmother who hardly ever came upstairs because it hurt her rheumaticky leg so badly.

"Grandmother!" cried Annette, and held out her arms.

Grandmother said nothing for a time; she sat down on the bed and stroked Annette's head until the child stopped crying.

"Listen, my child," said Grandmother at last, "when Dani was a baby we took him to the Church and by faith we laid him in the arms of the Saviour. Every day in prayer we have asked the Saviour to hold him safe in His arms. And even when Dani fell, the Saviour did not let go of him. His arms were underneath him all the time. Even if he had been killed he would have been carried straight home to Heaven. So let us dry our tears and go on trusting the Saviour to hold Dani, and do the very best for him."

"But why did God let Lucien hurt him so?" argued

Annette. " Grandmother, I hate Lucien so, I should like to kill him."

" Then you cannot pray for Dani," replied Grandmother simply. " God is Love, and when we pray we are drawing near to love, and all our hatred must melt away, like the snow melts when the sun shines on it in spring. Leave Lucien to God, Annette. He rewards both good and evil, but remember, He loves Lucien just the same as He loves Dani."

Grandmother kissed her and went away, and Annette lay thinking over Grandmother's words. The last remark she did not believe. It seemed impossible that even God should love cruel, ugly, stupid Lucien as much as good, sunny little Dani. But the first part she knew to be true, and it troubled her. She could not really pray for Dani and go on planning how to hurt Lucien. The two just did not go together; she wanted to pray for Dani, but if she did her hatred might disappear and she did not want that to happen at all—anyhow not before she had really had her revenge.

Well, in the meantime she would let Grandmother do the praying and she would go on planning her revenge.

Chapter Six

LUCIEN also lay in bed in the dark, with a hot throbbing head and eyes that could not shut, because each time he closed them he saw Dani just disappearing over the cliff. And it wasn't the ordinary cliff, it was a dark sheer cliff that had no bottom; you just went on falling for ever and ever.

Now and again he half fell asleep, but each time he awoke with a little cry of fear and his heart beating wildly, for his dreams were even worse than his thoughts. If only some one would come! It was so dreadful being alone. He wanted his mother, and he knew she had come in, for he could hear her moving about in the kitchen below. But he dared not call to her, for she must be so terribly angry that perhaps she was staying away on purpose. Besides, his sister might answer his call, and Lucien did not in the least want to see his sister. What she would say to him he dared not even imagine.

He began to think about tomorrow. He supposed he would have to go to school and Annette would have told everyone. Nobody liked him much in any case, ugly, bad-tempered and stupid as he was, but now they would all hate him. No one would be friends, or want to sit next to him in class, or walk home from school with him.

He heard steps on the stair, and his mother came into the room and sat down on the bed watching him with a worried frown.

All her heart went out to him in pity, and she longed

to comfort him, but she was dreadfully frightened. She was afraid of what the Burniers would do if Dani were badly injured; afraid of the law, afraid of doctor's bills that she could not pay. She dared not seem too sympathetic lest it should be said that she had taken her son's part. Besides, she felt it her duty to punish him somehow.

If she had been an understanding woman she would have seen that no punishment of hers was needed. She would have seen the long weeks of fear and loneliness and remorse that lay ahead of Lucien, and she would have known that her part was to comfort him and help him through them as best she might. But she was not very understanding.

"You are a naughty boy, Lucien," she said heavily, "and I do not know what is going to happen. If that Burnier child is badly injured we shall be ruined. We shall have to pay all the bills, and we cannot possibly afford it. I shouldn't wonder if we get the police after us. It's a terrible thing to have done, and I hope you are heartily ashamed of yourself."

Lucien was so very ashamed of himself that he didn't answer at all, which puzzled his mother very much, for Lucien was usually so quick to answer back and to stick up for himself. A silent Lucien was indeed a new thing.

"Well," she said at last in a gentler voice, "we must hope for the best! Tomorrow you could go and tell the Burniers how sorry you are, and perhaps they will forgive you."

She waited for his reply, but none came, so she said no more and left the room very troubled. She returned presently with a bowl of hot soup. It might be undutiful to comfort her son, but at least she could feed him.

Lucien took the bowl and tried to eat, but at the third mouthful he choked and handed it back to his mother. Then flinging himself down with his face buried in the pillows he cried again as though his heart would break. His mother said nothing, for she did not know what to say; but she stroked the back of his head gently, and then as his sobs grew quieter she crept away and left him to the night.

When he awoke next morning he could not remember what had happened, nor why his head ached and his eyes felt hot and heavy. Then it all came rushing back like a blow, and he remembered something else too. Today he had got to go to school and face the other children.

Dani might have died in the night and they would all know it was his fault.

He would not go, he would hide all day. It would not be very difficult. He would run up to the pinewoods and come back late in the afternoon, and no one would ever know. His mother would think he had been at school and no one from school would ask questions. He lived too far up the valley, and, besides, who cared? Of course someone would find out in the end, but today was all that mattered at the moment. He might feel different tomorrow, or Dani might be better; anything might happen later on, but today he would run away and hide.

He got up and went downstairs. Marie was in the kitchen. She had already eaten her bread and coffee and was getting ready to set out for the station. She tossed her head and turned away when Lucien came in, but Lucien did not look at her at all. He passed through the kitchen in silence, and went across to the stable to help his mother with the early milking.

She watched him with a troubled expression when he came in, but he said nothing. And sitting on his stool by the stove, eating his breakfast, he was still perfectly silent. At last he got up, buttoned on his coat, kissed his mother good-bye without a word and went off.

She stood watching him as far as the bend and then

waved to him. He waved back and waited round the corner until he was sure she had gone. Then turning on his steps he scudded up the hill as fast as his legs would carry him.

He ran very fast, and arrived breathless into the quiet coolness of the great pinewood that skirted the mountain. Here he was safe, for it was still early morning (school begins at 7.30 in Switzerland), so he sat down and began to think.

It was a beautiful pinewood and the trees wakening at the call of spring were surging with sap and scent. The sap burst from them and streamed down their grey trunks, and a sweet hot smell rose from the ground where the sun filtering through the boughs shone in patches on the pine needles. The forest seemed full of peace and cool light, and Lucien suddenly felt a tiny bit hopeful—as though one of the stray sunbeams had lost its way among the boughs and had pierced the misery in his heart.

He had no idea what he was going to do all day, and he had no food, as dinner was always provided for him in the school dining-room. But this strange feeling of hope made him feel sleepy, and because he had spent a broken, troubled night he stretched himself on the needles, well hidden by some wild raspberry bushes, and fell into a deep sleep.

When Lucien awoke, the sun was high overhead and the children down in the school were flocking out to their dinners. He wanted his dinner, too. But there was none to be had here in the forest, so he rose and wandered on up the hill, wondering whether some kindly farmer in one of the higher chalets might give him a drink of milk. And as he wandered he stuck his hands in his pockets and found his knife, drew it out, then began whittling at a piece of wood.

He had often done this before, though he had never

done anything serious. But now, with nothing to do, he decided to try to carve out the shape of a chamois, one of the wild mountain goats that live on the high precipices. He started off idly, chipping away at the block.

Very gradually it began to take shape under his fingers, and a strange excitement took hold of him. For the first time he forgot his misery and became absorbed in what he was doing. He could see the creature in his mind's eye, and his fingers followed his thoughts—a head, with beautiful curved horns and an eager tilted nose, was beginning to appear; then a lifted ear that had heard the horns of the huntsmen; then four slender hoofs, and a body poised for flight.

Lucien held it out at arm's length to inspect it. It was not perfect, though it was an unmistakable likeness, and Lucien himself had no idea how good it was. But for the first time since the accident he felt almost happy. He had found something he could do: stupid as he was, he could carve, and now he would not mind being alone again. And when the other children didn't want him he would come out to a quiet corner of the woods and see beautiful things and carve them. While he carved he could forget, and that was what he wanted more than anything. Whatever happened he could come away by himself and forget.

He climbed up the slope and looked down over the forest to the valley below. The sun was moving towards the western mountains, and far beneath he could see little dark specks running in all directions; the children were coming out of school. In another quarter of an hour or so it would be safe to go home.

He sauntered slowly back through the pinewood, for he must not get back too soon. The sun was shining on the other side of the valley now, and the pinewood was cool and dark and filled with little wakeful murmurs. Lucien kept his hand in his pocket with his fingers closed tightly over the rounded body of his chamois. It was a satisfying feeling.

He wondered rather dully what he would hear when he got home. Dani might have died; but Lucien pushed that thought away from him, for he dared not face it. He was probably just badly hurt, and into Lucien's mind there came a picture of Dani's white, scared little face looking up from the grass.

If only he could do something to make up. But he could think of nothing.

He walked into the chalet a little sheepishly, and his mother, at the sink, eyed him anxiously. She waited a little while for him to speak, but at last, unable to contain her curiosity any longer, she began to question him.

"Well," she began, "how did you get on at school today?"

"All right, thank you," answered Lucien.

"I've been down to enquire at the Burniers'," went on his mother, "and Annette and Monsieur have taken Dani to the doctor in the cart. They will not be back till late. The grandmother spoke very kindly, Lucien. They are good people and I think they will forgive you and not make the trouble you deserve."

Lucien didn't reply. The grandmother might forgive him, but he knew quite well that Annette never would.

"Did the schoolmaster know of what had happened?" asked his mother after a pause.

"Yes," replied Lucien.

"Did he say anything about it?" went on Madame.

"No," answered Lucien.

His mother was puzzled. She had had a miserable day thinking of what her son might be undergoing at school, but nothing seemed to have happened. He even looked slightly more cheerful than he had looked in the morning.

"I am going over to milk, Mother," said Lucien, and he

crossed to the stable with a sigh of relief. The stable was a refuge where he could get away from his mother's questions, and where the cows thought none the worse of him. He started quickly, and then, tilting the bucket, he drank about a pint of warm frothing milk straight off and felt better. He had had nothing to eat or drink since breakfast.

Tonight he would save some of his supper, and tomorrow he would go back to the woods again and spend another quiet, hidden day. He would do it every day till he was found out—and that might not be for a long time; he lived so far up the valley.

He took as long as he could over the milking and then sauntered back to the house carrying the pails. He reached the door at the same time as his sister, who had hurried up the hill and was flushed and breathless.

"You little coward, Lucien!" she exclaimed by way of greeting. "Fancy missing school like that! What has he been doing all day, Mother? You should have made him go!"

Her mother turned round indignantly. "What are you talking about, Marie?" she asked sharply. "Of course he's been to school. He's only just come in. Leave the poor child alone and get on with your work."

"Indeed!" exclaimed Marie. "Well, if he's only just come in, I should dearly like to know where he's come from. I happen to have met the schoolmaster on my way up from the station. He was weeding his vegetable patch. He looked over the fence and called out to me. 'Where is Lucien?' he says, 'and why has he not come to school? Is he not well?'—and I answered, 'He's well enough, and he shall come tomorrow, if I have to drag him!' So now you know, Lucien! Goodness knows where you've been today, but tomorrow I shall take you to school myself."

"Fancy you lying to me like that, Lucien," cried his

mother angrily. "You *are* a wicked boy. I do not know what to do with you. The master must deal with you." And because she was so worried, and because her boy had deceived her, she threw her apron over her face and began to cry.

Lucien sat down by the stove in bitter, sullen silence. Everything and everyone seemed against him. His only hope of escape had been taken from him; tomorrow he would have to go to school and Annette would be there. If he had gone today she would not have been there.

He picked up a large chip and began whittling away with his knife, and once more his fingers felt for the wooden chamois in his pocket.

Chapter Seven

Dani lay in the cart on a sack stretched across a soft mattress of hay and gazed up at the sky, where tiny white woolly clouds floated like sleepy lambs in a blue meadow. He would have liked to look over the sides of the cart, but this was impossible, for he could not sit up; so he looked at the sky instead, and Annette described the scenery and events of their journey. Dani's leg ached badly, and he was inclined to be fretful; when the cart jolted he squealed. But Annette soothed him with her talk, and it was still nice being so important.

"We are at the top of the village now, Dani," said Annette, "just passing the church, and there is Emil the dustman's son driving the cows out of the churchyard. Some naughty person must have left the gate open."

"Are the cows trying to go into church?" enquired Dani with interest.

"No," replied Annette. "They were trying to jump over the wall, but it was too high; they were jumping over the gravestones instead. Here we are at the Infant School, Dani, and there is the mistress scrubbing her step. I suppose it is her cleaning day and she has given all the infants a holiday. I wish the master had cleaning days. Oh! here is the mistress coming towards the cart. She has seen us, and I expect she wants to know how you are, and here come Madame Pilet and Madame Lenoir. They have seen us, too. They were washing their clothes in the fountain."

Annette was right; they certainly wanted to know how Dani was. For in a tiny village news travels fast, and is much talked of and long remembered because there is so little of it. The postman's wife had heard some of the story from Lucien's sister when she 'phoned for the doctor, and the station-master's wife had heard the rest from Marie while she waited for the early train, and by now everyone knew about it and everyone was talking about it and everyone wanted to find out more.

They all crowded round the little cart, loud in their indignation against poor Lucien.

"He is a wicked boy," said the Infant School mistress; "I shall warn the little children not to have *anything* to do with him!"

"I shall *not* allow Pierre to play with him," said the postman's wife. "He has a cruel heart. You can see it in his face. I am sorry for his mother." She spoke in a superior way, and thought proudly of her own merry-faced, freckled Pierre, who was one of the best-loved boys in the village.

Dani's father flicked his whip a little impatiently, and called back that they must not keep the doctor waiting. So the women stood back and the cart lumbered on slowly over the cobbles. Then they all drew together again and started talking in the middle of the road with their heads very close together.

The cart jolted on and the sun rose higher. The horse did not mind in the least about keeping the doctor waiting, and Annette had plenty of time to describe the scenery to Dani as they made their slow way to town.

The journey passed pleasantly. They left the great roaring waterfall behind on their right hand, and went on up a broad road, with young mountain ash trees on either side. They passed through the saw mills with machines smelling of sawdust, and then on between fields of young crocuses, until houses began to appear. Annette told Dani that they were coming to the town.

"Tell me about the shops!" exclaimed Dani eagerly. He had been to the town only three times in his short life, and thought it the most wonderful place in the world.

You would not have thought it much of a town, for there was only one narrow street of shops—but they were very nice shops. There was the cake shop with its windows packed with flat fruit tarts and piles of gingerbread cut into every imaginable shape; and the clothes shop with its display of flounced embroidered national costumes. Best of all was the wood carvers' shop with its rows of carved cuckoo clocks, and the old men who opened their mouths wide and cracked nuts in their wooden teeth. Annette was quite breathless with describing the beauties of this shop, when at last they drove up in front of the hospital.

It was only a little hospital really, but to Annette and Dani it seemed enormous. The patients all lay out on sunny balconies, and the door was wide open. Father jumped down from the driver's seat, tied the reins to the fence and went in. A few minutes later he returned with two men and a stretcher.

Dani, on his stretcher, was laid on a wooden bench in the outpatients' hall, with Father sitting at his head and Annette at his feet. The quiet strangeness of the place and the queer, clean smell awed them all into silence, so Dani watched the nurses instead. They wore long white aprons and lace caps; Dani thought they were exactly like the angels in Grandmother's big picture Bible.

They waited for a very long time. Father and Annette nodded and dozed. Dani flung his arms above his head and fell into a deep sleep.

He was woken by the doctor who bore down on them

very suddenly and seemed in a great hurry. He was an elderly man with a large black beard and a gruff voice. Annette felt afraid of him.

Everything seemed to happen very quickly after that. Dani was hustled off on a trolley to have the bones of his leg photographed, which was interesting, and he wanted to know whether he would be allowed to keep the photographs to hang up in the sitting-room. Then he was trundled back, and the doctor pulled the bad leg till Dani screamed with pain—at which point the photographs were brought along, not looking in the least like Dani's legs.

But the doctor seemed pleased with them. He studied them deeply and nodded his head wisely. Then he turned to Father and remarked,

"This child should stay in hospital. He has broken his leg very badly."

But Annette's father refused utterly. He was not going to leave his little son to this man with his black beard and his hands that were none too gentle. "We will look after Dani at home," he said firmly; "surely that is possible?"

The doctor shrugged his shoulders. "It is possible," he replied, "but I think he would be better here. I cannot come so far; you would have to keep bringing him in."

"I do not mind bringing him in," said Father obstinately, and Annette stole her little hand into his big one and gave it an approving squeeze. She, too, wanted Dani at home.

The doctor shrugged his shoulders and spread out his hands. Dani was once more trundled off by a nurse in a great hurry, and this time he did not come back for more than half an hour.

When at last he was returned to them, he looked sleepy and strange and could remember absolutely nothing but a queer smell, and it was Annette who discovered that he was encased from his waist to his knee in a fine white plaster. She pointed it out to Dani, who stared down at himself in astonishment.

"Why have I got to wear these hard white trousers?" he asked at last, and then, without waiting for a reply, he announced that he did not like the doctor's big black beard and he wanted to go home.

Annette did not like it either, and they all wanted to go home—Annette because she was hungry, Dani because he was tired, and Father because he was thinking about his cows; and when the doctor came back to take a second photograph, Dani and his family were nowhere to be seen. Only in the far distance a sprightly horse was making his way towards home as fast as possible, trundling a hay-cart and three passengers behind him.

"Stupid creatures," muttered the doctor. "I suppose they thought I was never coming back. Now I shall have to trudge up some out-of-the-way mountain for the best part of a day and visit the child. They did not even wait to hear when they were to come again."

Truth to tell they had quite forgotten to ask. Father remembered just as he was unreining the horse.

"Annette," he called back, "we never asked how long Dani had to wear his plaster."

"Never mind," Annette answered. "You will be passing again with the cheeses in a week's time and you can call in and ask them. You may be sure it will have to stay on as long as that. Leon at school had one on his arm and he wore it six weeks."

"So he did!" replied Father, reassured. "Then I won't go back now, for it is getting late, and that doctor is nowhere in sight." He hoisted himself on to the driver's seat and called out "Huh, Coco!" And the horse, with his nose turned in the right direction at last, made off at a fast trot.

They reached home at five o'clock and Dani was put to bed on the sofa so that he might not feel lonely; and Annette slept on a mattress beside him lest he should wake in the night and want her. Here Dani stayed for weeks, with his leg on a pillow, and the whole household moved round him.

Annette stopped going to school altogether for the time being, and gave herself up to being Dani's slave. She told him all her stories over and over again and played games with him all day long. Grandmother cooked wonderful little meals in the kitchen to tempt the appetite of the 'poor little sick boy'—whose appetite didn't need tempting in the least, for he was almost as jolly and cheery and hungry on his couch as he was off it; and when Annette was busy he would lie flat on his back on the verandah bed and sing like a happy lark.

Dani's leg, however, was very slow in healing. On several occasions the doctor climbed the mountainside to visit him, but he seemed grave and puzzled. Then, when the narcissi were beginning to sprout in the fields, and the farmers were talking about taking the cows up the mountain, Dani went back to hospital and they took the plaster off. Then it was that the doctor broke the news to Dani's father, that, as he had feared all along, Dani would not be able to walk straight. The bad leg was decidedly shorter than the good one.

So in very low spirits Monsieur Burnier went to the carpenter and asked him to make a tiny pair of crutches; then he visited the cobbler with a pair of Dani's boots and asked him to make one sole an inch and a half thicker than the other.

The carpenter and the shoemaker were dreadfully upset. The carpenter carved fascinating little bears' heads on the handle of the crutch in order to bring a smile to Dani's face, and the cobbler returned the boots stuffed with chocolate sticks, and in both cases their efforts were a great success. Dani looked upon his crutches as a new toy, along with all the other things provided to make him happy. All the village was prepared to love Dani, and care for him.

Chapter Eight

Just as the village rallied round Dani and did all they could to comfort him, even so they shunned Lucien, and did all they could to show their contempt.

For a few days he was actively tormented. The master made a speech about him in school and held him up as a public example of a bully and a coward. The children chased him out of the playground and threw mud at him. But they soon gave that up and simply settled down to ignore him.

Lucien had never been liked, for he was bad-tempered, clumsy, and ugly, but he had gone about with the crowd, and joined in with their games. Now he had to settle down to a terrible, dull, lasting loneliness. Nobody wanted to play with him. When teams were picked he was always left till last. There was one extra single desk in the class-room; it automatically fell to Lucien; all the others sat in couples.

Even the tiny children got out of his way, for their mothers had warned them to have nothing to do with him. " He is a cruel bully and may harm you as he harmed little Daniel Burnier," said the mothers—and the little ones looked on him as a sort of ogre, and ran away as he approached.

Down at the village shops they handed him his goods across the counter silently; the milkman never chatted to him, and the grocer's wife never slipped trimmings of gingerbread into his hand—as they did to other children.

They never spoke unkindly to him; they just took no notice of him.

And Lucien, too shy to make any attempt to overcome their dislike, drifted into a lonely little world of his own. He walked to and from school alone, he shopped alone, and in the playground he usually played alone. It was not that the children would not have him, for children forgive and forget quickly; it was simply his shame that kept him from joining in. Always he saw hostility and dislike in their faces, and imagined they were thinking of crippled Dani, and gradually he grew to be afraid of them, from the old milkman right down to the youngest child in the school. He was afraid of their scorn and dislike.

For Lucien himself was always thinking of crippled Dani. The thought haunted him, and he yearned to ask Annette what the doctor had said. But Annette had neither looked at him nor spoken to him since the day of the accident, and he dared not speak to her.

At home his mother found him more silent but more hard-working, for he had suddenly discovered that only by hard work could he forget his loneliness. So instead of indulging in his old lazy habits he threw himself into the work of the farm with an almost desperate energy. His mother praised him loudly, and his sister became kinder, for she herself was a hard-working girl and Lucien's laziness had always annoyed her exceedingly.

But there was one place, and one only, where Lucien was completely happy—and that was in the forest. Here the kindly trees shut him in, and the world that disliked him was shut out. Here Lucien fled whenever he had any spare time, and, squatting against a tree-trunk or boulder, he would carve away at his little figures and forget everything else in the joy of his craftsmanship.

Now high up on the borders of the forest there stood a small chalet where a very old man lived by himself. He had retired there long ago and he lived alone with his goat, his hens, and his cat. He was a queer old man. Everyone in the village was afraid of him, and when he came down on rare occasions to shop, the children ran indoors. They called him the old man of the mountain; some said he was a miser, some said he was hiding from the police, and others said he was crazy and malicious. Be that as it may, no one had ever been inside his home, and no one ever passed that way after dark.

Lucien had wandered farther than usual one half-holiday and sat as usual intent on his work. He was carving a squirrel holding a nut between its paws when he suddenly became aware of heavy breathing behind him, and turned quickly to see the old man of the mountain looking over his shoulder.

He was certainly a terrifying sight. His huge matted grey beard covered his chest, and his hooked brown nose gave him the look of some fierce old bird of prey. But as Lucien gazed up, startled, into his eyes he noticed that they were bright and kindly and full of interest, and he decided not to run away after all. Besides, his great loneliness made him less afraid than he would have been otherwise. This old man might be queer, or even wicked, but at least he knew nothing about Lucien's past.

So Lucien said, "Bonjour, Monsieur," as boldly as he could, and waited to see what would happen next.

The old man put out a hand like a brown claw and picked up the little carved squirrel. He examined it and turned it over several times; then he remarked in a piping voice,

"You carve well for a child. Who is your master?"

"Monsieur, I have no master. I taught myself."

"Then you yourself are a good master, and you deserve proper tools. With a little training you might start to earn your living. There is life in this squirrel."

"Monsieur, I have no tools, nor have I the money to buy them."

In reply the old man beckoned with his claw, and Lucien, feeling like someone in a dream, rose and followed him through the dim wood. They climbed some way in silence until they came to the borders, where stood the tiny chalet where the old man lived.

There was no outhouse except for a wood barn where the hens roosted, and the goat shared the kitchen with the old man—so did the marmalade cat who sat washing herself in the sunshine. The bedroom was also the hayloft, and the old man slept on sacks laid across the goat's winter provender.

The kitchen and living-room was poorly but strangely furnished. There was the stove, the milking bucket and stool, the manger, the table, one chair and a cheese press. But all round the walls, out of reach of the goat, were shelves covered with carved wooden figures, some beautiful, some grotesque, but all the work of a real artist.

There were bears and cows and chamois and goats, and St. Bernard dogs and squirrels. There were little men and women, gnomes and dwarfs, and dancing children. There were boxes with alpine flowers carved on their lids, and dishes with wreaths carved round the rim. And best of all there was a Noah's ark with a stream of tiny animals prancing in. Lucien could not take his eyes off this; he stared and stared and stared.

"Just a hobby of mine," said the old man. "They keep me company on winter evenings. Now, boy, if you will come and visit me from time to time, I will teach you the use of the tools."

Lucien looked up eagerly. His whole face was alive, and he no longer looked ugly.

"Did you say, Monsieur," he asked hesitatingly, "that perhaps I might soon earn my living?"

"In time," said the old man, "yes. I have a friend who sells woodcraft at a good price. He sells many of my little figures—but some I get fond of and prefer to keep. In a short time he would start selling your best work for you—you will soon do much better with my tools than with your knife."

Still Lucien gazed up at him. His heart was singing with gratitude because this old man seemed to care for him, and wanted to take an interest in him. Here at last was somebody of whom he need not be afraid, and who thought well of him. He took hold of the old man's hand impulsively.

"Oh, thank you, Monsieur," he cried. "How very good you are to me!"

"Zut!" said the old man, "I am lonely, and I have no friends. We can carve together."

"And I, too," repled Lucien simply, "am lonely, and have no friends."

As Lucien walked home through the forest his brain was seething with ideas, but there was one big idea more important than all the others. He would make a Noah's ark for Dani like the old man had done, with dozens of tiny figures—lions, rabbits, elephants, camels and cows, and Mr. and Mrs. Noah, and when it was quite perfect he would walk round to the Burniers' chalet and give it to Dani as a peace-offering. Surely no one could give Dani a better present than that! And after that, perhaps—perhaps they might even allow him to be just a tiny bit friendly with Dani again.

His heart beat fast at the mere thought. For two whole hours he had been completely happy, and his happiness lasted all the way through the forest until the trees parted and he saw the village spread out at his feet. Tomorrow he would have to go back to school. Tomorrow he would feel lonely and frightened again. But today he had kept company with a friend.

So three times a week after school Lucien bounded through the still pine forest, and sat on the step of the old man's chalet and worked at his Noah's ark. It was a wonderful thing to use those tools with their sharp blades and easy curves—very different from the old clasp-knife.

The old man marvelled at the boy's skill. The Noah's ark family grew and multiplied. Every visit Lucien thought of some new beast to carve, and the procession grew longer and longer.

There was another excitement for Lucien just about now. An inspector came to the school and set a handcraft competition for the children. The girls were to see who could enter the best specimen of knitting, or needlework, or lacemaking, and the boys the best specimen of wood-carving. Many of them whittled away at wood in their spare time, and some were well on the way to becoming skilful.

"But no one is as skilful as me," whispered Lucien to himself, as he plodded home alone; "I shall win the prize. And now they will know that I can do something well, even if I am stupid at lessons, and even if no one will play with me."

And Lucien sang on his way home that day. He saw himself walking up for his prize in front of the amazed school. Perhaps they would like him better after that.

He would carve a horse with a flowing mane, in full gallop, with tail outstretched and nostrils dilated. Lucien loved horses; the old man had carved one like that and Lucien had admired it tremendously. The Noah's ark would be finished very soon and then he could start on his little horse.

He ran straight up to the old man's house to share the

news. The old man was pleased, and as sure of Lucien's success as Lucien was himself.

"But why try a horse?" he asked. "You could submit your Noah's ark. It is very well done for a boy of your age."

Lucien shook his head. "That is a present," he said firmly.

"A present? Who for? A little brother?"

"For a little child who has hurt himself and cannot walk."

"Indeed? How did he do that?"

"He fell over the ravine."

"Poor little fellow! How did that happen?"

Lucien did not answer for a moment. But the fact that this old man had befriended him and been nice to him made him want to speak the truth. He looked up at last and said—

"It was my fault that he fell. I dropped his kitten over and he tried to get it."

He could have bitten his tongue out, when he had said it. Now the old man would hate him and drive him away like everybody else.

But he didn't. Instead the old man said very gently,

"So that is why you said you had no friends?"

"Yes."

"And you are trying to make amends to the child with this toy?"

"Yes."

"You are doing a good thing! It is hard work to win back love. But do not be discouraged. Those who persevere find more happiness in earning love than they do in gaining it."

"I don't quite understand you," said Lucien, thoughtfully.

"I mean that if you spend your time putting the love

of your heart into your deeds for those who are not your friends, you may often be disappointed and discouraged, but if you keep on you will find your happiness in loving, whether you are loved back or not. You may think it strange that I who live alone and love no one should say this; but I believe it all the same."

That evening the Noah's ark was finished and Lucien, with a flushed face and a hammering heart, set off for the Burniers' chalet to leave it on his way home.

When he came within sight of the chalet, he hid behind a tree in a panic. What would he say? How would he break the silence? If he could see Dani alone it would be easier, but Annette was always with him out of school hours.

Surely they would forgive him when they saw the Noah's ark! If only they would forgive him and give him a chance he would gladly spend the rest of his life trying to make up. And torn between hope and fear Lucien came out from behind his tree and walked towards the chalet.

Dani's bed had been carried in; Annette sat alone on the verandah patching her father's jacket elbows. Lucien swallowed hard, walked up the steps and held out the Noah's ark.

"It's for Dani," he whispered hoarsely, and then his words stuck in his throat, and he stood waiting with his eyes fixed on the ground.

Annette took the Noah's ark from him, her face white with fury.

"You *dare* come here!" she burst out at last. "You *dare* offer presents to Dani! Go away and don't you ever come here again!"

And as she said it she flung the Noah's ark with all the strength of her young arm into the woodpile below. All the little animals lay scattered on the logs.

Lucien stared at her for a moment, then he turned and

stumbled down the steps again. His efforts had been all for nothing. He would never be forgiven; it had all been one long waste of time.

And then the words of the old man came into Lucien's mind like a tiny ray of light in his angry, bitter heart.

"Those who persevere find more happiness in earning love than in gaining it."

Well, perhaps it was true. He had certainly not gained anything, but at least he had been happy making the Noah's ark, and thinking of Dani's pleasure. Perhaps, if he persevered, and went on putting his love into his work, some day someone would accept it and love him for it.

He did not know . . . but he would not despair just yet.

Chapter Nine

In Switzerland, when the grass begins to grow long in the fields, the cows go up the mountain for the summer and feed in the high pastures, while the hay ripens in the valleys. Monsieur Burnier had led away his cows, but Lucien did not go up the mountain, for the Morels possessed only four cows, which they farmed out with another herd for the summer, so until hay-making started in the fields around his home Lucien had plenty of time after school and sought out the company of the old man of the mountain nearly every day.

His horse was nearly finished, and a beautiful little bit of work it was for a boy of Lucien's age. It was a larger figure than he had attempted before, with a flying mane and little hooves that hardly seemed to touch the ground. As you looked at it you thought of speed and slender grace; Lucien spent hours over it, and studied every horse in the neighbourhood so that he might perfect each muscle.

He still had plenty of time because the competition was not to be judged till the end of the hay-making holiday, but already the school children were beginning to make guesses about the results.

Most of the boys backed Michel, the milkman's son, who had carved two bears climbing up a pole. He had worked hard, and it was a good piece of work; but they could easily have been mistaken for dogs or any other animals, thought Lucien, looking at them silently, while the other children were loud in their admiration.

Nobody could mistake his horse, thought Lucien; it was a horse and nothing but a horse; but no one suspected that he might win the prize, because no one except the master knew he had entered for it. He had been too shy to tell them; too afraid of their scornful faces and their lack of interest. But now, looking at Michel's bears, he knew that he would win. There was not another entry to touch his. And he saw himself walking up for the prize, and every eye turned on him in admiration and astonishment; and then they would all be interested and want to see his horse—and then perhaps they would like him better. His face flushed a little at the thought.

There was more discussion about the girls' entries. Marcelle from the shop made beautiful lace, and had done so from the time she was five years old. Jeanne's mother was a dressmaker and she had been brought up in the trade, but Annette was a skilled little knitter. Grandmother had taught her when she didn't go to school. She was entering a dark blue jersey she had knitted for Dani to wear on Sundays and festivals, with alpine flowers knitted in bright colours round the neck and waist. She had not yet finished it, but it was a promising article, and everybody praised it as she sat working away in the playground.

"I think you are sure to get the prize, Annette," said several of her friends. "It is harder to do a pattern like that than to make lace like Marcelle. Everyone says so."

And Annette was hopeful too. She wanted so badly to win that prize. It would make up a little for getting such disgracefully low arithmetic marks. And how pleased and proud Grandmother, Father and Dani would be!

However, unlike Lucien, she had very little time, for her after-school hours were always busy. And now the hay-making holidays had begun, and all children worked in the fields from dawn to dusk, side by side with their elders.

A good deal of friendly arranging had to be done at hay-making time. A neighbour who had grown-up sons to help on his farm went up to the high pastures to look after the Burnier cows, while Monsieur Burnier came down to cut the hay on his own slopes; and after he had finished he always went over and cut the hay in the little meadow that belonged to the Morels, because Madame Morel was a widow, and Lucien not yet old enough to wield a scythe.

Monsieur Burnier cut his own meadow first, and then went off to cut the Morel patch, leaving his family to gather in his own swathes. Madame Morel had been a little nervous this year, lest by way of revenge he should refuse to come, but she need not have worried. She woke one morning and from her window saw him hard at work, his brown body stripped to the waist swinging in rhythm with the scythe.

"Hurry, Lucien," she called, "Monsieur Burnier is already mowing in the meadow—run out and start on the haycocks."

Lucien shuffled sheepishly into the field and bade Monsieur Burnier good morning with his eyes on the ground. He hated having to work with the man he had wronged and kept as far away from him as possible, and Monsieur Burnier had no wish to hold any conversation. It was one thing to mow a neighbour's meadow, but quite another to chat with the boy who had crippled his little son.

Annette arrived at noon with her father's dinner done up in a handkerchief. She also took no notice of Lucien, and when he saw her coming he slunk away into the house.

It took Monsieur Burnier three days to mow the Morel meadow, and the third day was the last day of the holidays. Lucien and his mother and sister were working hard to clear the field before Lucien went back to school. They were all in the meadow when Annette appeared as usual with her bundle and gave it to her father. She was in a hurry, for the next day the children had to give in their entries for the handwork competition, and Annette still had the finishing touches to put on her jersey.

"I do wonder if I shall get that prize," said Annette to herself. "I do want it so—but even if I don't, Dani will look sweet in the jersey."

The meadow lay at the back, and on her way home Annette passed the front of the house. It was a very hot day, and Annette was thirsty. The door leading from the little verandah into the kitchen stood invitingly open.

"I will go in and have a drink from that tap," thought Annette, climbing the verandah steps—and indeed there was no harm in that. Before the accident Annette had run in and out of the Morel kitchen as though it were her own.

She climbed the verandah steps, and having reached the top she suddenly stopped dead and stood quite still, staring and staring.

There was a little table set against the outer side of the balcony, with some carving tools and chips of wood on it. And amidst the chips was the figure of a little horse at full gallop, with waving mane and delicate hoofs.

Annette stood for a full five minutes gazing at the little creature, lost in thought. Of course it was Lucien's entry for the competition, and the deceitful boy had never even told anyone he was submitting an entry, or that he knew how to carve at all.

It was almost perfect; even Annette's jealous eyes could see that. If he gave it in he would win the prize easily; no one else could touch him.

And when he won the prize, everybody would begin to

admire his work and perhaps they would begin to like him for it. Perhaps they would begin to forget that he had crippled Dani.

And if Lucien won the prize he would be happy. He would walk up to receive it with his head in the air, and to see Lucien looking happy would be more than Annette could bear. Why should he be happy? He deserved never to be happy again. He should not be happy if she could help it. She had arrived just at a fortunate moment.

The table stood at a level with the verandah railings, and a gust of wind fluttered the shavings of wood. A rather stronger gust of wind could easily blow the light little model over; no one would ever suspect anything else when they found the little horse smashed and trampled in the mud below.

Annette put out her hand and pushed it over. It fell on to the stones with a little crack and Annette bounded down the steps and stamped on it—anyone could accidentally tread on something that had blown over the verandah railing.

So Lucien's horse lay in splinters among the cobbles, and Annette walked slowly home.

But somehow the brightness had gone out of the day, and the world no longer looked quite as beautiful as before. Annette wondered why, for no cloud had passed in front of the sun.

It was not long before she came in sight of her own chalet, and as she turned the corner Dani saw her and gave a loud welcoming shout. Something very, very exciting had happened, and if he had been an ordinary little boy he would have raced to meet her—but, being Dani, he merely came hobbling up the hill as fast as he could, doing enormous leaps on his crutches.

" 'Nette, 'Nette," shouted Dani, his eyes shining, " I

think there's been some fairies in the wood pile; I made a little house down behind the logs, and I found a tiny little elephant with a long trunk, and I looked again and I found a camel with a hump, and a bunny rabbit with long ears, and cows, and goats and tigers and a giraffe with ever such a long neck. Oh, 'Nette, come and look at them; they are so beautiful, and no one but the fairies could have put them down behind the woodpile, could they?"

"I don't know," answered Annette, and her voice sounded quite cross. Dani looked up at her in astonishment. She didn't seem a bit pleased at his news, and it was almost the most wonderful thing that had happened to him since he had found Klaus in his slipper on Christmas morning.

However, when she saw them she was sure to be pleased; she didn't yet know how beautiful they were. He hopped valiantly along, rather out of breath, because Annette was walking faster than she usually did when he was beside her.

He dragged her to the woodpile, and dived behind it, reappearing with the procession of carved animals, arranged on a flat log. He looked anxiously at her, but to his great disappointment there was no sign of surprise or pleasure in her face.

"I expect some other child dropped them, Dani," she said crossly, "and anyhow it's nothing to make such a fuss about; they are not all that wonderful—and you're too big to believe in fairies."

She turned away and went up the steps, hating herself. She had been unkind to Dani, and spoiled all his happiness. How could she have spoken to him like that? What had happened to her?

But deep down inside her she knew quite well what had

happened to her. She had done a mean, deceitful action, and her heart was heavy and dark at the thought of it. All the light and joy seemed to have gone out of life.

And now she could never get rid of it or undo it. She ran upstairs to her bedroom and, flinging herself on the bed, burst into tears.

Chapter Ten

LUCIEN ran home from the hayfields with a light heart that evening. He had worked hard, and his body was tired, but his little horse was waiting for him; tomorrow he would carry it to school and everyone would know that he could carve.

Up the steps he bounded, and then stopped dead. His horse had gone; only the tools and the chips lay on the table.

Perhaps his mother, who had come home earlier, had taken it in. He hurled himself into the house.

"Mother! Mother!" he cried, "where have you put my little horse?"

His mother looked up from the soup pot. "I haven't seen it," she replied; "you must have put it somewhere yourself."

Lucien began to get seriously alarmed.

"I haven't," he answered; "I left it on the table, I *know* I did. Oh, Mother, *where* can it be? do help me find it!"

His mother followed him at once. She was just as keen on Lucien's winning the prize as he was himself, and together they hunted high and low. Then Madame Morel had an idea.

"Perhaps it has fallen over the railing, Lucien," she said, "go and search down below."

So Lucien went down, and searched, but he did not

search for long. He found it all too quickly—the muddy, scattered splinters that had once been his horse.

He gathered them up in his hand and took them to his mother—her cry of disappointment brought Marie running out, and both of them stood gazing in dismay.

"It must have been the cat," said Marie at last; "I am sorry, Lucien. Haven't you anything else you could take?"

His mother said nothing except "Oh, Lucien!"—but the voice in which she said it meant quite a lot.

Lucien said nothing at all. He just went indoors and looked at the clock on the wall.

"I'm going up the mountain," he said, in a voice that tried hard to be steady. "I won't be home for supper."

He ran down the balcony steps and up through the hayfield where the swathes lay like waves in a green sea. His mother watched him with a troubled face until he disappeared into the forest. Then she went back and wept a few tears into the soup pot.

"Everything goes wrong for that boy," she murmured sadly. "Will he never succeed in anything?"

Lucien trudged through the forest, seeing nothing. Little grey squirrels leaped from branch to branch and flung acorns at each other, but he took no notice of them, because he could think of nothing at all but his lost prize and his bitter disappointment—how someone else would get the honour that he deserved, and he would continue to be disliked and despised. And he would never get another chance to show them how good he was at carving. No one would be interested—unless he had won that prize.

He had reached a clearing in the forest, and he could see over the tree-tops to the ranges of white peaks beyond the mountains that shut in his immediate valley.

"I wish I could go right away," he thought to himself, "and start all over again where nobody knew me, or knew what I'd done. If I could go and live in another valley, I shouldn't feel afraid of everybody as I am here."

His eyes rested on the Pass that ran between two opposite peaks and led to the big town in the next valley where Marie worked. The sight of that Pass always fascinated him; it seemed like a road leading into a world beyond, away from all that was safe and familiar—an eerie spot where daring travellers had been caught in blizzards and perished in the waste. Twice he had crossed it himself, but that was in summer when the sun was shining and the Pass strewn with flowers. Now, it was bright with the last rays. To Lucien's gaze it suddenly seemed like a door of escape from some prison—a door he must pass through alone, to find release in a land of sunset.

Lucien saw the old man as he left the wood, long before the old man saw him. For the old man was sitting at his front door, his chin resting on his hands, gazing intently at the mountains on the other side of the valley. Not till the boy was quite close to him did he look up.

"Ah," said the old man in his deep mumbling voice, "it is you again. Well, how goes the carving, and when are you going to win that prize?"

"I am not going to win the prize," replied Lucien sullenly; "my horse is smashed to pieces. I think the cat knocked it over the railings, and someone trampled on it."

"I am sorry," said the old man gently, "but surely you can enter something else! What about that chamois you carved? That was a good piece of work for a boy."

Lucien kicked at the stones on the path savagely.

"I did it without proper tools," he muttered, "and they would think it was my best work. No, if I cannot enter my little horse, I will enter nothing."

"But does it matter what they think?" enquired the old man.

"Yes," muttered Lucien again.

"Why?"

Lucien stared at the ground. What could he answer to that? But the old man was his friend, almost the only friend he had. Maybe he had better try to speak the truth.

"It matters very much," he mumbled, "because they all hate me and think me stupid and bad—and if I won a prize, and they saw I could carve better than any other boy in the valley, they might like me."

"They wouldn't," he said simply. "Your skill when used for your own ends will never buy you love. It may buy you admiration and envy, but never love. If that was what you were after, you have wasted your time." Lucien continued to stare at the ground. Then suddenly he looked up into the old man's face, his eyes brimming with tears.

"Then it is all no good," he whispered haltingly. "There seems no way to start again, and to make them like me. I suppose they just never will."

"If you want them to like you," replied the old man steadily, "you must make yourself fit to be liked—and you must use your skill in loving and serving them. It will not happen all at once; it may even take years—but you must persevere."

Lucien stared up at the old man.

"You wonder why I should talk of loving and serving others, do you?" enquired the old man. "You were right to wonder such a thing. It is a long story, too."

"Well," admitted Lucien, "I was thinking that it must be difficult to love and serve people when you live alone up here and never speak to anyone but me."

The old man sat silent for some moments, looking out over the far rock peaks which the sunset was touching with gold; then he said:—

"I will tell you my story, but remember, it is a secret. I have never told it to another living soul. But you have trusted me, and I will trust you, too."

Lucien flushed. Those were good words; even the prize and his disappointment seemed to matter less. It was better to be trusted than to win prizes.

" I will start at the beginning," said the old man simply. " I was an only child, and there was nothing in the world my father would not give me. If ever a child was spoiled, it was I.

" I was a clever boy, for all my selfishness, and when I grew up I was given a good post in the Bank. I worked hard and climbed to the top. I fell in love with a girl, and married her. God gave us two little sons, and for the first few years of our life together I believe I was a good father and a good husband.

" But I got in with a bad lot of friends who flattered me and invited me to their homes. They were interested in gambling, and they drank heavily. I admired them and began to learn their ways. Gradually I began to spend more and more money on drink and gambling.

" I need not tell you much about those years. Our money began to dwindle away, and people began to talk about my bad ways. The Bank manager warned me twice, but the third time he dismissed me.

" I tried to find another job, but my story was known, and no one would employ me. I tried to earn money on the gambling tables, but I never had any luck. I lost the little I had.

" My wife went out daily to work, as well as looking after the house and the boys, but she could not earn enough to keep us all. One day she came and told me we were in debt, and could not pay.

" I was desperate for money, to pay our debts and to buy myself more drink. I had not worked in the Bank as a high and trusted official for nothing. I knew the ways of it inside out, and I decided to commit a robbery.

" My plan, which was a skilful one, succeeded; but it was

not quite skilful enough. I was discovered, and tried, and as I could pay nothing back, and the robbery had been a heavy one, I was condemned to a long term of imprisonment.

"My wife had been ill for many weeks. She was hopelessly overworked, and ate next to nothing so that there should be enough for the boys. She visited me in prison, but I could see she was dying, and the end came all too soon.

"I remember little about the months that followed. I seemed numbed and lost in despair. I had only one comfort. All my life I had loved woodcarving, and in my spare hours in the common-room they let me have my tools and whittle away at bits of wood. I grew more and more skilful, and a kindly warden used to take my work out and sell it in the town. I earned a little money in that way and saved it eagerly. One day I supposed I should have to start again.

"The day came sooner than I expected. I was summoned to the governor and told that I had been granted a reprieve for good conduct. In three weeks' time I should be a free man.

"I wandered back to the prisoners' common-room hardly knowing whether to be pleased or sorry. I supposed I should be glad to leave prison, but where should I go, and how start life again? One thing I had determined. My boys should never see me again, or know where I was. They had been adopted by their grandparents, and I knew they were growing up into fine, intelligent boys with good futures ahead of them. They should never be branded with my bad name or shadowed by my past. To them I would be as though I were dead.

"Beyond that I knew nothing. The governor offered to help me start afresh, but I wanted to leave no traces of where I was going, and refused his help. When the day of my release came, I walked out with my little sum of money in my pocket and took the first train up into the mountains. It was there that a peasant took me on as a herdsman. He trusted me, and I began to see his faith in the Living God. I, too, began to believe in the love and mercy of God.

" But after four years my master began to grow weak and ill. He visited the doctor, but nothing could be done for him. I cared for him for a year and his son often came to see him, but at the end of that time he died, and I was left alone.

" So I lost my only friend, although his son was very good to me. His son was a rich man by now; he sold the cows and gave me this chalet for my own. So I bought a goat and a few hens, collected my few possessions and came here and have lived here ever since.

" I have only one friend—the shopkeeper in the town who sells my carvings; he sometimes gives me news of my sons. They have grown up into good men and they have done well; one is a doctor and one is a businessman. They do not know that I am alive, and it is better so. I have nothing that I could give them, and my name would only disgrace them.

" But through the lives and the words of my master and my wife, I too have come to believe in the love and mercy of God and the forgiveness of sins. I cannot pay back the people I robbed, for I don't know who they are, but nevertheless I am working hard. I have now saved nearly as much money as I stole, and when I have saved the whole sum I will seek for some person or some cause who truly needs it—and to them I will pay my debt.

" You tell me there is no way to start again, but you are wrong. I have sinned far, far more deeply than you have done, and have suffered in a way that a child like you can know nothing about. But I believe that God has forgiven me, and I am spending my days working to give back what I owe to mankind, and striving to become what God meant me to be. It is all I can do—it is all anyone can do. The past we must leave to God."

The goat had come up and rested its brown head on the old man's knee; and it butted at the old man's waistcoat to remind him it was milking time. Lucien rose to go.

He walked home slowly. "I am spending my days working to restore what I owe . . . striving to become what God meant me to be." He thought about it a lot—so much so, that the matter of the prize seemed quite small, and he found that he had stopped minding so very much; well, he couldn't restore Dani's leg, but one day he might get the chance to do something great for him—and as for the second part, he could at least try to be a nicer boy. There was his mother, for instance—she was miserable, because his carving was broken. Well, he would be brave, and show her he didn't mind, and then she would be happy again.

As he left the wood he could see the orange lights in his chalet windows, warm and welcoming, shining out into the summer dusk. The crickets were chirping in the fields, and the newly cut hay smelt sweet and strong.

He ran lightly up the chalet steps and kissed his mother, who was standing on the balcony watching for him.

"I'm hungry, Mother," he said gaily. "Have you saved my supper?"

And over the top of his bowl of soup he smiled at her, and the shadow passed from her eyes as she smiled back.

Chapter Eleven

THE next morning, Dani woke in great excitement. It was the day of the prize-giving, and he hopped about impatiently until it was time for him to be off, dressed in all his Sunday glory of black velvet and embroidered braces. His father pulled the cart, and Annette walked beside him, dull and sad and rather cross.

What could be making Annette dull and sad on such a morning? The sun was shining, the river was glistening, and Annette was going to win a prize. There was everything to make them happy, and anyhow Dani never felt sad or cross except when he had a pain in his leg.

"Have you got a tummy-ache, 'Nette?" asked Dani, suddenly.

"Of course I haven't, Dani," answered Annette, peevishly. "Why should I have a tummy-ache?"

"I just thought you might," explained Dani. "Oh, 'Nette, look, there's a blue butterfly sitting on my shoe."

But Annette did not even turn round to look at the blue butterfly. She walked on, staring at the ground. Whatever could be the matter with Annette?

Already the schoolroom was filling when they arrived. The desks had been stacked on one side and the children's work was laid out on long tables, and a very pretty show it made. Mothers and fathers walked round admiringly, while the children jostled and nudged each other, pointing and chattering like magpies.

There was the knitting table covered with brightly

coloured specimens of children's work; there was the embroidery table gay with embroidered aprons and belts; there was the lace-making table and the crochet table. On the other side was the boys' work with specimens of woodwork and carving carefully arranged.

Pierre, the postman's son, was there, standing bright-eyed and confident close to his own piece of work—a wooden inkstand with a bear standing over the inkwell. The snout was a little crooked, and the bear's flanks were definitely fatter one side than the other; still, it was a bear, there was no mistaking it, and it was a good piece of work for a child of Pierre's age.

Lucien was there too, wandering round by himself as usual, for his mother was behindhand with the hay, and had not come down. He stared gloomily at the inkstand and compared that heavy stuck bear with his own sprightly horse. If only that accident had not happened the children would have been standing round him instead of round Pierre. He felt a great angry stab of jealousy for Pierre, who was clever, and beautiful to look at, and good at games, and who now was going to win the prize that belonged to him—Lucien. He drifted away into a corner by himself and stared gloomily at the crowd.

Annette, surrounded by a chattering group of friends, was strangely silent. Some thought she would get the prize, some backed up Jeanne. There was much guessing, much running to and fro, and much putting together of heads, some saying one thing and some another. Only Annette, usually so gay and talkative, said nothing.

Dani, his hand clasped tightly in his father's, hopped round inspecting everything, and everyone made way for him and gave him a kind word as he passed. Then, having seen all there was to see, he took up his stand at the end of the long table close to Annette's entry, so that he might be right on the spot when the prizewinner was announced.

Being a very small boy, there was nothing to be seen of him above the top of the table but his unruly thatch of sun-bleached hair and his round blue eyes, very wide open and anxious.

The door opened, and a sudden hush fell on the chattering crowd; the man from the town by the lake had arrived to judge the work. The children and parents stood quietly against the walls as the tall man walked slowly round, picking up and examining first one thing and then another. He praised a great many objects and spoke kindly of all. He had come prepared to see a good exhibition, he said, and he was not disappointed. He looked through the children's exercise books, piled on a table in the far end of the room, and talked about their work. A kind, patient man, but very slow. All the children wanted to know was, who was going to get the prize?

Well, he was going to make up his mind about the girls first; he walked over to Marcelle's lace and examined it carefully, and then he went back to Annette's knitted jersey, and stood turning it over in his hands, and the room was so silent that you could have heard a pin drop.

Then suddenly the silence was broken.

"My sister made that," said a clear, distinct child's voice.

The big man jumped and peered over the end of the table. He saw a small round face lifted to his, alight with hope and eagerness, and just for a moment he wondered why he suddenly found himself thinking of a young beech tree bursting into leaf in the sunshine.

"Then your sister is a very clever girl," replied the big man gravely, after a few seconds' pause; and as he spoke he noticed the crutches.

"I think it's the very best of all, don't you?" went on Dani earnestly, quite unconscious that everyone in the room was listening to him—unconscious of anything but his great longing for Annette to win.

As a matter of fact the big man had not quite made up his mind when Dani first spoke, but now he suddenly felt quite certain. He did not realize that Dani had really decided for him.

"Yes, I do; I think it's the very best," answered the big man, and Dani, without an instant's hesistation, turned round on his crutches and faced his sister, who was blushing deeply at his bad behaviour.

"You've got the prize, 'Nette," called Dani, and everybody burst out laughing and started clapping. And so, in this highly irregular and unexpected fashion, the prize-winner for the girls was announced.

Pierre won the boys' prize; it was announced properly after a suitable speech to which none of the children listened. Then there was tea—rolls and gingerbread and macaroons, and then Pierre went home with a crowd of admiring friends. They all played leap-frog in the square, and all bought chocolate sticks for Pierre by way of congratulation—after which he went home and ate the fruit tart his mother had cooked him for his supper, and was sick in the night.

Lucien went down to the village alone to fetch the loaf, and when he came back past the school the playground was deserted and the children had all gone home. He climbed the hill slowly, but it was not the weight of the bread-basket on his back that bowed his shoulders, and made him walk with his eyes on the ground.

For Lucien was very unhappy. Why was it that one day it seemed easy to be brave and cheerful, and the next day it seemed impossible to be anything but angry and jealous? Yesterday, on the way home from the old man he had thought that he would not mind seeing Pierre get the prize, but today he hated Pierre. The old man had talked about striving to become what God meant you to be, but somehow, however hard you tried, it seemed impossible to change yourself for long.

And yet the old man had become different, and Lucien found himself wondering how. The old man had talked about God; perhaps God could make nasty people nice if they asked Him. Lucien felt he didn't know very much about God—and anyhow God was probably very angry with him for being so wicked to Dani.

But could God really love him much?—and surely God wouldn't forgive a sin like that in a hurry?—and even if God did, nobody else would. His unhappiness came surging back over him and he gave a great sniff, and kicked angrily at the stones on the path.

He was passing the corner where the path divided not far from Annette's chalet, and as he branched off towards his own home his ear was caught by the sound of a little child singing, and he turned to look.

Dani and Klaus were sitting on a hollowed-out pile of new hay, like two birds in a nest, and Dani's bright head was bent low over something, as he crooned joyfully away to himself. His crutches lay on the ground beside him.

Urged on by his great loneliness, Lucien drew a step nearer and stood watching. And suddenly his cheeks flushed with pleasure and he drew a sharp little breath. For Dani had dug out a sort of cave in the wall of his hay nest, and inside it were grouped all the little wooden animals that he had carved with such care.

"So she *did* give them to him," thought Lucien to himself, with a little thrill of happiness. "And he *does* like them!"—and aloud he added, "What are you playing at, Dani?"

Dani jumped, and looked up and saw the boy who had tried to kill his kitten. His first reaction was to seize Klaus round the middle tightly and say, "Go away, you horrid boy!"

But as he said it, even he, although he was only five years old, could not help noticing that Lucien looked very unhappy, and unhappiness was a thing that his friendly little heart could not bear. So, still holding the struggling and indignant Klaus very tightly, he added cautiously after a moment's pause:

"I'm playing with my fairy Noah animals, but 'Nette said I mustn't talk to you."

"But I wouldn't hurt you," answered Lucien very gently, "and I'm very sorry about your leg. That's why I made those animals for you."

"You didn't make them," answered Dani cheerfully; "I found them behind the woodpile—the fairies put them there."

Lucien was just about to answer, when Annette's voice came sharp and shrill from the door of the chalet.

"Dani," she shouted, "come in at once; supper's ready."

Lucien turned away. "So she didn't tell him," he thought, rather bitterly. Still, it was nice to know that Dani loved them and played with them. One day he might get a chance to explain, and then perhaps he and Dani would be friends. He climbed the path between the hayfields slightly comforted.

Dani hopped into the kitchen, climbed into his seat, and hugged his empty tummy joyfully while his nose twitched like a rabbit's at the smell of Grandmother's potato soup.

"'Nette," began Dani, "Lucien said that he made my fairy Noah animals; but he didn't, did he? The fairies put them behind the woodpile, didn't they? He wasn't speaking the truth, was he?"

"I've told you not to talk to Lucien, Dani," said Annette rather crossly. "He'll only hurt you again. He's a horrid boy."

"Yes," answered Dani, "and I only talked to him a

teeny, weeny bit; but he didn't, did he, 'Nette? Tell me!"

Annette hesitated. She was a truthful child, and she did not want to tell a lie; but if Dani knew, he would be so grateful that he would forgive Lucien at once, and go and thank him—and then there was no telling where it would all end. They would be fast friends in a few minutes. It was hard enough as it was to make Dani be unfriendly with anybody, but if he knew about the animals it would be quite impossible.

"You know you found them in the woodpile," she replied, looking away, "so how could he have made them? Don't be silly, Dani!"

"Well, he said he did," answered Dani, "but I knew he didn't. It must have been the fairies, mustn't it, 'Nette?"

"Oh, I don't know, Dani," replied poor Annette, wearily. "How you do chatter! Eat your soup up quickly. It will be all cold."

Dani obediently buried his nose in his bowl, but Grandmother, whose dim old eyes saw more than most people's, looked very hard at Annette. She too had heard and wondered at the story of the animals in the woodpile.

And Annette, knowing that Grandmother was looking hard at her, went very red, and going over to the stove pretended to help herself to some more soup. But she only took a little, for somehow she wasn't a bit hungry. For the day she had looked forward to for so long was all spoiled. She had got the prize she wanted so badly, but it hadn't made her a bit happy. In fact, she was perfectly miserable.

She washed up the supper things in silence, tucked up and kissed a warm, sleepy Dani, and slipped out alone into the summer dusk. She usually loved being alone on summer evenings—just her and the still blue mountains

—alone to look at what she wanted, and to think and play what she liked and go where she pleased.

But tonight it was different. The rushing of the stream and the chirping of the crickets, even the lazy goat-bells, seemed strange unfriendly sounds, and the shadowed fields seemed lonely and frightening—she didn't want to think, because she could think of nothing but that little smashed horse lying trampled on the ground, and of the light that had died in Dani's face when she had spoken so crossly to him.

"I wish I could tell someone!" thought Annette. "It wouldn't be so bad then—I wish Mummy was still alive; oh, I wish, I wish, I *wish* I hadn't done it!"

Chapter Twelve

THE summer lengthened into autumn, the cows came home down the mountain, and the second mowings were gathered in. Then Annette pulled Dani in his cart up to the nut bushes, and they gathered baskets full of hazel nuts. Dani was growing taller every day, and by October the village cobbler had to make him a new pair of boots. He went to the Infant School, too, every day, and Monsieur Burnier paid two big boys one franc each a week to pull him home in the cart.

And now Christmas had come round again; the snow lay over a foot deep on the chalet roofs, and Father had had to dig a path from the front door to the main sledge track. The little stream was silent and frozen, its tiny trickle muffled by the snow on the boulders, while icicles hung like bright swords from the rocks.

Christmas was a very special time to Dani, for all the great events of his life had happened at Christmas. His mother had died on Christmas Eve, and though Dani had never known and missed her, yet even he sensed a certain gentle sadness in his father's face and felt a special tenderness towards him and Annette.

It was his own birthday, too, and this year he was six. He had thought for a long time about being six, and he expected to wake up quite a new child on the morning of Christmas Eve. So it was a little disappointing to find, as he lay in the shuttered darkness, that he really felt no bigger, or stronger, or more majestic than the day before.

Then he remembered that he was going to see the Christmas tree in the church, and Grandmother had made a special cake for his birthday, and after that there was no room for disappointed thoughts any longer.

And of course, according to Dani, Christmas was Klaus's birthday, too. It wasn't really Klaus's birthday because Klaus must have been at least a fortnight old when she crept into Dani's shoe, but Dani had never thought of that. For him Klaus had begun early Christmas morning, straight from a reindeer sledge, a white ball of Christmas magic, begotten of stars and snow. So Annette bought twenty centimes' worth of red ribbon at the village shop, and Klaus went about over the Christmas season with a large bow on her neck, looking very handsome and uncomfortable, inclined to scratch anyone who paid any attention to her.

Best of all, it was the birthday of the Lord Jesus, and although Dani did not talk about it very much, he thought about it a lot. It made him strangely happy to know that he shared the birthday of the perfect Child.

"What could I give to the little Lord Jesus for a birthday present?" he had asked, resting his elbows on Grandmother's knee, and looking up into her face.

"You can give your own self to Him," Grandmother had answered, pausing a moment in her knitting. "And you can ask Him to make you very loving and obedient. That will please Him better than anything."

So throughout Christmas Dani tried to be loving and obedient, in order to please the Child whose birthday he shared, and his love just overflowed to everyone. He tidied Grandmother's workbox, and wiped the dishes for Annette; in the afternoon he went out to the shed and visited the cows in turn, murmuring Christmas messages into their silky ears. And at the end of the day, when he knelt to pray, he whispered, "I hope I am giving You a happy birthday, little Lord Jesus."

And so Dani had a perfect birthday, and when evening came and it was time to wrap up and go down to the church he was bubbling over with joy.

To begin with, there was the ride on the sledge sandwiched between Father and Annette, with the cold air making his nose feel as though it wasn't there. It was almost full moon, and the white mountains looked quite silver. All the trees in the forest were weighed down with snow, and the lower branches trembled as they rushed past, powdering Dani's little hood.

Out of the wood, over the bumpy little bridge and down across the last field with a cold rush, and there was the little church with the rosy light of hundreds of candles streaming from the windows and door, and the muffled forms of the villagers greeting each other in the porch. Then Dani, blinking and glowing with sudden warmth, was carried up the wooden aisle in Father's arms and placed on the front bench with the other children from the Infant School—thirty little rosy-faced children in woolly hoods gazing open-mouthed at the tree; only three days ago it had been weighed down with snow in the cold forest near Dani's house. Now it was jewelled and decked and glistening, festooned with oranges, chocolate sticks, and shining gingerbread bears.

The older school children sang a carol first. It was a sweet, sad song, supposed to be the mother Mary singing to the sleeping Child on her knee—

Dormez, dormez sur mes genoux;
O, petit Jésus, endormez-vous !

Annette was singing it with the others, and her thoughts flew back to that Christmas night when she had first held

Dani in her arms. How they had welcomed him and watched him—yet none but His mother had welcomed the little Saviour. "They laid Him in a manger; because there was no room for them in the inn."

The carol finished, the older children went back to their seats and the Infant School trotted to the front. Dani got left behind because crutches do not move as fast as sturdy legs encased in woollen stockings and boots; but they waited for him, and everyone in the audience smiled as he reached his place with a final hop and turned his radiant face upon them.

Voici Noël,
O douce nuit!
L'étoile est là
Qui nous conduit.

Dani glanced up at the bright star on top of the Christmas tree and saw it reflected on the shining gingerbread bears below, and forgot what he was singing because he was wondering which particular bear was going to belong to him. There was one which looked as if it was laughing —the baker had accidentally given a little twist to its snout. Dani thought he would like that one, and laughed back at it.

As the babies strayed to their seats with backward looks at the tree, the old pastor climbed into the pulpit. He had been pastor in that village for forty-five years, and everybody loved him. His shoulders were bowed and his skin tanned, for he still climbed the mountains in all weathers to visit his scattered flock. His beard was so long and white that Dani, with his head full of the tree, got him mixed up in his mind with Father Christmas, and wondered why he was wearing a black coat instead of a red one.

Annette listened rather dreamily to the story she knew so

well, half thinking of other things, until the old man suddenly repeated the words that had always haunted her every Christmas since the night when she had imagined herself the mother Mary, with all doors shut against her.

"'There was no room for them . . .'—no room for *Him*!"

In the unhurried manner of very old people, he repeated it three times, and each time Annette thought the words sounded sadder. How quickly she would have opened her door!

"And yet," went on the old man, "tonight the Saviour is still standing at closed doors—there are still hearts that have never made room for Him. This is what He says:—

"'Behold, I stand at the door, and knock; if any man hear My voice, and open the door, I will come in. . . .'

"What will you do about Him this Christmas? Will you open the door, or will you leave Him standing outside? Will those sad words be said about you, 'There was no room for Him'?"

"I should like to ask Him to come in," thought Annette —"I wonder what it all means. The clergyman spoke about asking Him to come into our hearts. I wonder if I could ask Him into *my* heart."

Just for a moment Annette thought it rather a nice idea, and looked round to see whether other people thought it was, too. And as she looked round she suddenly noticed Lucien sitting on the other side of the church, with his mother and sister.

And as she caught sight of him she realized that she couldn't ask the Saviour to come into her heart because her heart was so full of hatred for Lucien—and of course the Saviour would not want to come into an angry, unforgiving heart. Either she would have to forgive and be kind, or else the Lord Jesus would have to stay outside.

And she didn't want to forgive and be kind. Not yet.

There was something else, too. She had broken Lucien's carving and let him think it was the cat, and cheated him of his prize. If the Lord Jesus came into her heart, He would have something to say to her about that, and she did not want to listen.

The sermon was over, but she had not heard much of it because she had been so busy with her thoughts. So busy was she that Dani had to nudge her to make her see that it was time for him to go up and get his bear.

The church was full of a low murmur of conversation, and the little ones were surging forward to the tree. Monsieur Pilet, the woodcutter, was distributing bears. Dani gave his sleeve a firm tug and pointed to the top bear who was laughing at the Christmas star.

"Please I want that one," he whispered, "that one up there; please I want it very badly!"

And because of the crutches and because it was Christmas, Monsieur Pilet, the woodcutter, moved the ladders, moved the children, and moved the lower lights, and with immense difficulty and inconvenience he climbed up and took hold of the bear that Dani wanted. And Dani was dragged home through the starlight and the snow with the bear of his choice held close to him; every time he looked down at that merry curved snout he chuckled gleefully, as though he and his bear had some private Christmas joke between them that nobody else knew about.

Chapter Thirteen

CHRISTMAS Day was over, and Dani was asleep with his flushed cheek pillowed on his arm. Father was across in the stable, and Annette and Grandmother sat one each side of the stove. Grandmother was knitting white woollen stockings for her grandchildren, and Annette was supposed to be patching her pinafore—but actually her pinafore had slipped to the ground and she was simply staring in front of her with her chin resting on her hands.

"Annette," said Grandmother suddenly, without looking up from her knitting, "have you had a happy Christmas?"

"Yes, thank you, Grandmother," replied Annette rather dully, because that was what she supposed she ought to say. And then she added suddenly, "Grandmother, what does it mean when it says that Jesus knocks at the door of our hearts?"

"It means," said Grandmother, laying down her knitting, and giving Annette her whole attention, "that the Saviour sees that your life is full of wrong things and dark thoughts. He came down and was crucified so that He might bear the punishment of those wrong deeds and those dark thoughts instead of you. Then He rose again so that He could come into your life and live in you, and turn out all those wrong thoughts, and think His good, loving thoughts in you instead. It is like a man knocking at the door of a dirty, dark, dusty house, and saying, 'If you will let me in I will take away the dust and the darkness and make it beautiful and bright'. But, remember, He never *pushes* in—He only asks if He may come in. That is what knocking means. You have to say 'Yes, Lord Jesus, I need You and I want You to come and live in me'—that is what opening the door means."

Annette's eyes were fixed on Grandmother; there was a long, long pause.

Annette broke the silence.

"But, Grandmother," she said, drawing her stool nearer and leaning against the old woman's knee, "if you *hated* someone you could not ask Jesus to come in, could you?"

"If you hate someone," said Grandmother, "it just shows how badly you need to ask Him to come in. The darker the room, the more it needs the light."

"But I couldn't stop hating Lucien," said Annette softly, fingering her long plaits thoughtfully.

"No," said Grandmother. "You're quite right. None of us can stop ourselves thinking wrong thoughts, and it isn't much good trying. But, Annette—when you come down in the morning and find this room dark with the shutters closed, do you say to yourself, 'I must chase away the darkness and the shadows first, and *then* I will open the shutters and let in the sun'? Do you waste time trying to get rid of the dark?"

"Of course not!" said Annette.

"Then how do you get rid of the dark?"

"Well, I pull back the shutters, of course, and then the light comes in!"

"But what happens to the dark?"

"I don't know; it just goes when the light comes!"

"That is just what happens when you ask the Lord Jesus to come in," said Grandmother. "He is Love, and when love comes in, hatred and selfishness and unkindness will give way to it, just as the darkness gives way when you let in the sunshine. But to try to chase it out alone would be like trying to chase the shadows out of a dark room. It would be a waste of time."

Annette did not answer—only she sat for a little time staring at the wall, and then she picked up her pinafore with a sigh and worked at it in silence. After a while she rose, kissed her grandmother goodnight very quietly, and went up to bed.

But she could not go to sleep for a long time. She lay in the dark, tossing and turning and wondering.

"It's quite true," she said to herself. "If I asked Him to come in, I should have to be friends with Lucien, and I don't want to be. And I suppose I should have to tell how I broke his carving, and I could never, *never* do that. I shall just have to try to forget about the knocking—and yet I feel so terribly miserable."

She thought that she could forget all about it and find some other way of being happy. So she turned over her hot pillow, and made herself count the goats running to pasture until she fell asleep.

The next morning she dressed and went down to breakfast rather depressed, only to find everything in a turmoil, because Dani had lost Klaus, and was refusing to eat his breakfast until she was found.

"She always wakes me in the morning," explained Dani excitedly. "She comes and purrs at me—but this morning she wasn't there. She went out last night before I went to sleep and she hasn't come back."

Dani's distress was terrible to behold and the whole household was moved. Father did an outside tour of the barns, Grandmother rummaged about in the kitchen, and Dani explored perfectly impossible places. Annette went upstairs and searched the bedrooms, but it was all in vain. Klaus was nowhere to be found. Father had last seen her stalking towards the barn with her tail in the air, picking her way gingerly across the soft snow—and no one had seen her since.

It was a wretched day. Dani broke down at dinner, and between his sobs declared that he could not eat anything because Klaus was hungry; his tears trickled down into his soup and no one had any power to comfort him, although neither Father nor Grandmother seemed particularly worried. " She will come back, Dani," said Father quietly. " She is only hiding for today."

There was no sun either. Grey clouds hung low, hiding the mountains, and fresh soft snow began to fall. At night it would harden into a crust and next day would be dangerous for walking. Father pulled on his cape and got out the big sleigh to haul in logs. Grandmother went to sleep in the armchair by the stove, and Dani came and leaned against Annette and looked up into her face.

" 'Nette," he said plaintively, " I want to go to bed."

" Why, Dani?" asked Annette, astonished. " It's ever so early—only just beginning to get dark; and you haven't had your supper!"

" But I want to go to bed, 'Nette," persisted Dani. " You see, I want it to be time to say my prayers."

Annette gave a little laugh.

" You don't have to go to bed to say your prayers, Dani," she replied. " You could say them just as well now, and then have your supper and go to bed at the ordinary time."

But Dani shook his fair head.

"No," he said, "I want them to be my proper prayers in my nightgown. Please put me to bed, 'Nette."

"Oh, all right," answered Annette, beginning to unbutton his jersey, "but you know, Dani, it doesn't really make any difference being in your nightgown"—and then she kissed him because his small face looked so terribly sad and his mouth drooped so at the corners.

And when he was safely buttoned into his white starched nightshirt he knelt down and folded his hands and prayed for Klaus.

"Dear God," he prayed, "please bless Klaus. Please find her and bring her back to me quickly. Don't let her be cold, or hungry, or frightened. Show her the way home tonight. Please, please, dear God. Amen."

"Aren't you going to pray for anyone else?" protested Annette, in a slightly shocked voice.

"No," replied Dani, getting up from his knees in a hurry, "not tonight. I don't want God to think of anyone but Klaus tonight!" And then, thinking that he was being perhaps a little unkind, he added, "*You* can say the other people later."

And, having committed Klaus into the hands of the heavenly Father, Dani climbed into bed with a peaceful heart, and pillowed his cheek on his hand. But he opened his eyes and said drowsily, "'Nette . . ."

"Yes," answered Annette.

"You'll wake me when she comes, won't you?"

"When who comes?"

"Klaus, of course!"—and with that Dani fell asleep.

Annette wandered round the room restlessly, and then because her cheeks felt hot and because she had been indoors all day, she opened the door and went out on to the balcony.

It had stopped snowing; a west wind was soughing up the valley, blowing the fresh snow across the old with a sound like a gentle sea—already it was piling in drifts against the walls of the chalet. It was not a bitterly cold wind—it felt pleasant on her hot cheeks, and she decided to go for a walk up to the stream bed. She might meet Klaus.

Chapter Fourteen

She wandered quite a long way and at last she reached the little bridge that crossed the stream. The railings were hung with icicles and the stream was almost silent—only a whispering runnel deep below the white boulders told that the stream still lived.

It was very still up there. The wind had dropped and it had begun to freeze—the little bridge was treacherously slippery and Annette, with her thoughts far away, never noticed the sheet of ice below the soft fall—until her foot slipped and she stumbled forward with a little cry of pain.

For a moment the pain in her ankle made her feel faint and sick, and she lay for a minute or two in the snow without moving. Then she tried to rise, but sank down again with another cry, for she had sprained her ankle badly, and could not stand on it at all.

For a few minutes she felt terribly frightened. She was alone on the mountainside, and no one was likely to come down that lonely forest path that night. It was getting colder and colder; unless she could reach shelter she would certainly freeze to death.

Then she remembered that there was a chalet a little farther up the mountain round the bend in the path, just inside the forest. A young woodman and his wife lived there; if she could drag herself on her hands and knees to their door they would take her home on their sledge. It was not very far. She would start at once.

She began crawling through the snow painfully enough,

dragging her poor swollen foot behind her. It ached dreadfully at every jolt, and before long she began to get terribly tired. Her hands kept sinking into the snow, and her eyes filled with tears; would she ever get there?

She had reached the hairpin bend in the path where the forest sprang up, and now to her relief she could see the chalet, not very far away, with one little light in the window. She felt she could go no farther, and sank down in a drift to rest a little; but she soon began to feel cold and braced herself to struggle on.

Foot by foot she advanced, until after what seemed hours she reached the steps of the little house. She gave a low cry, hoping that someone would come out and carry her up them, but no one came. So she struggled up herself and sank down in an exhausted heap on the doorstep.

Then with a sigh of relief she stretched up and knocked on the door.

There was no answer. The little house seemed as silent as the snow and the windless woods. Annette reached up again and knocked as loud as she could.

But there was still no answer; nothing stirred in the little house.

In a frenzy of fear she staggered up on one foot, and beat on the door until her fists were sore, shouting at the top of her voice, and rattling the latch. Then, as the horrid truth dawned on her, she sank down on the steps and burst into frightened tears. The door was locked and the house was empty. The little light had only been left on to scare thieves. There was no one there at all.

For a few moments panic seized her—for she was a mountain child and had often heard of people being frozen to death in the snow. But then her panic left her and she began to think rapidly and reasonably.

If they had left the passage light on they probably meant to come back that night.

But if they had gone down to the valley they might be a long time coming, and then perhaps it would be too late. Already she could feel the cold creeping into the tips of her fingers.

Perhaps if she rested a little she might be able to crawl back.

But the next chalet was a long, long way down, and the drifts were soft and deep.

Anyhow she would wait a little and then try. It was her only chance.

As she sat there waiting she thought of the Christmas talk. She knew now, for the first time, what it felt like to knock at a closed door and get no answer.

She had knocked for only a few minutes. But the Lord Jesus went on knocking for years and years—she knew He did.

She had stopped knocking because she knew the house was empty. But just supposing Monsieur and Madame Berdoz had been sitting inside all the time—just supposing they had heard her knocking out in the night and had looked at each other and said, " Somebody's knocking, but we won't let them in just now—we'll pretend not to hear —we won't take any notice!"

How angry she would have been with them—how much she would have hated them for being so unkind!

Yet that was exactly how she was treating the Lord Jesus—and He didn't hate her. He still loved her dearly, or He wouldn't still go on knocking and still want to come in. Grandmother had said so.

She was thinking so hard about this that for a moment she almost forgot her fear and loneliness. But now she suddenly lifted her head and strained her ears, for surely she heard a sound.

A very gentle sound, but one that all mountain children

knew well. The sound of skis running through soft snow; and then—the sound of a boy's voice singing.

Someone was coming down through the wood on skis—in a few seconds they would curve round the bend and shoot right past the front of the chalet. If they were going very fast they might not see her. . . .

A little figure came into sight swaying towards the valley as he took the curve with a thin veil of soft snow flung up around him. Annette kneeled upright and shouted at the top of her voice.

"Help!" she cried, cupping her hand in front of her mouth. "Stop and help me!"

The skier, with a sudden outward twist of his body, turned and brought his skis to a standstill. Then he unstrapped them and ran lightly up the slope towards her.

"What's the matter?" he cried, "and who is it? Are you hurt?"

It was Lucien. He had been up the mountain to visit his old friend, and now he was on his way home. He had been startled by Annette's cry, and when he saw who it was kneeling there in the moonlight he stood still and stared as though he had seen a ghost.

But Annette was too pleased to see anyone to care about who it was. Just for a moment she forgot everything except that she was found and saved, and to her grateful eyes Lucien might have been an angel straight from Heaven.

"Oh, Lucien!" she cried, in a rather shaky voice. "I *am* so glad you've come. I've hurt my foot, and I can't walk and I thought I might freeze to death before Monsieur and Madame Berdoz came home. Can you take me home, Lucien? I'm getting so cold."

Lucien's big mountain cloak was round her in an instant. He squatted down beside her, and rubbed her cold hands.

"I can't take you on the skis, Annette," he said gently, "because you're too big to carry. But I can be home in five minutes now and then I'll come straight back with the big sledge and a rug. I'll have you at your chalet in less than half an hour."

And inside himself his heart was so full of sudden joy that he felt he must run and shout and sing. His dream had come true. He was doing something useful for Annette—she needed him. Now perhaps she would forgive him and forget that terrible quarrel.

"Won't you be cold without your cloak, Lucien?" asked Annette in a small, exhausted voice.

Lucien promptly took off his jacket and wrapped it round her head, and wished he might give her his shirt as well—although it wouldn't have been the slightest use. He could feel the bite of the frost on his body, and sped back over the snow, bracing his muscles and drawing in deep icy breaths as though with the pain of that cold air he was paying the price of some great sin. He had his skis on in a trice, skimmed the curve like an arrow released from a bow, the joy in his breast glowing so that he was almost unaware of his numb body, until he stumbled into his own front door and his mother cried out at the sight of his bare arms and blue nose!

Annette, left alone, snuggled up in the warmth of Lucien's rough cloak. He would be back in about twenty-five minutes and in those twenty-five minutes there was a good deal to make up her mind about.

First, she was safe. Lucien had come out of the wood just at the right moment, and he had heard her cry. So all the time she had thought she was alone the Saviour outside the door had been caring for her and had sent Lucien to save her.

Secondly, she had discovered about closed doors. She was not quite sure yet just what would happen when she opened the door, but one thing she was quite certain about. She would not leave the Saviour outside any longer. She leaned her head against the snowy step-rail and closed her eyes.

"Lord Jesus," said Annette, "I'm opening the door now—I'm sorry it's been shut such a long time and You had to wait so long—please come in now. I'm sorry I've hated Lucien—please make me love him, and if I've got to tell about that little horse please make me brave enough; and thank You for sending Lucien to find me. Amen."

And so the Lord Jesus who had been waiting outside the door of Annette's heart and life for such a long time, came in, to forgive her sins and to make her good. There was no one there to see that wonderful thing happening—even Annette didn't really feel any different. But up in Heaven that night Annette's name was written in God's Book of Life, and the angels rejoiced because another child on earth had opened the door and made room for the Saviour.

Chapter Fifteen

"WELL," thought Annette, "I've done it, and now I know what's got to happen."

She found her heart beating very fast, and she looked up at the vast starry sky and the great mountains to steady herself. How big they were, how old and unchanging! They made her and her fears feel very small and unimportant. After all, it would soon be over and forgotten about, but the mountains and the stars would go on and on and on for ever.

A small black figure appeared, running round the curve in the path dragging a sledge behind him. He had procured another coat, and was so out of breath with hurrying that he could hardly speak.

"Come on, Annette," he gasped. "I've brought the big sledge so there's plenty of room for you to stretch out your leg. We'll be home in a few minutes."

He held out his hand to help her rise, but she drew back—"Just a minute, Lucien," she said, in a hurried, rather shaky voice; "I want to tell you something before we go home. Lucien, it wasn't the cat that knocked over your horse that day. It was me. I did it on purpose because I didn't want you to get the prize—because you hurt Dani; and I'm sorry, Lucien."

Lucien stood and stared at her, too surprised and, strangely enough, too happy to speak. For instead of feeling angry he felt tremendously relieved. Annette had done something wrong as well as he, and if he had to forgive Annette, perhaps it would be easier for Annette to forgive him. Of course a little smashed horse was nothing compared with a little boy's smashed leg, but even so it seemed to bring them somehow nearer together.

But he couldn't put all that into words, so he just gave a gruff little laugh and said shyly, "Oh, it's all right, Annette. You needn't bother. Get on the sledge." Then he tucked the cloak round her, sat down in front of her, and together they sped down the mountain side and arrived at the Burniers' front door powdered all over with the snow that flew up from the runners.

Annette climbed the steps on her hands and knees and stood on one leg in the door. Then she looked at Lucien, who was turning away slowly with the sledge.

She had opened the door of her heart to the love of the Lord Jesus, and that meant opening the door to Lucien as well, for the Saviour's love never shuts anyone out.

"Come up, Lucien," she called. "Come in and see Grandmother; she will be so pleased that you found me."

And she opened the front door as wide as it would go, and she and Lucien went in.

Grandmother jumped up with a cry of joy at the sight of Annette. They had been very anxious and Father had gone up the mountain to search for her. She was opening her mouth to be cross when she noticed the lame foot, so she shut her mouth, helped Annette on to the sofa instead, and went to look for cold-water bandages.

But as she turned she noticed Lucien standing shy and irresolute on the threshold, and for a moment they stood looking at each other. Grandmother's dim old eyes could read the faces of children like open books, and here she saw such repentance, such hungry appeal, such timid hope and dawning courage as she had never seen in any child's face before. She put both hands on his shoulders and drew him to the warmth and blaze of the open stove.

"You are welcome, my child," she said firmly. "Come and sit down and eat with us."

The door opened again, and Father entered, shaking the snow from his cloak. He had guessed Annette was safe for he had seen the sledge and the forms of two children whizzing across the fields. When he had heard her story and scolded her a little for going so far alone at night, he too sat down by the open stove, and Grandmother served out hot chocolate and crusty bread thickly spread with golden butter to them all—and on top of each hunk she placed a thick slice of cheese full of holes, and everyone sat munching in silence.

A sleepy, contented silence! The warmth of the stove after the night air made them all feel drowsy. Lucien sat blinking at the flames and wished that this moment could last for ever—when suddenly the silence was broken by a queer scratching noise on the door.

"It's Klaus!" shouted Annette, and sprang forward—but her bad foot held her back, and it was Grandmother and Father and Lucien who all opened the door at once.

Klaus marched into the room with her tail held proudly erect and in her mouth a perfectly new blind, tabby kitten. She took no notice of any of them, but walked straight across to the little bed where Dani lay sleeping, and jumped up on to the feather quilt. She dropped her precious burden as near as possible to the tousled golden head, and then hurried back to the door and miaowed.

"She'll be coming back with another," said Father letting her out.

"Then we had better leave the door open," said Grandmother and she hugged her shawl tightly round her shoulders and asked Lucien if he would kindly fetch the chamois skin and put it over her knees. Then they all sat shivering in an icy draught until Klaus reappeared in a great hurry, deposited a smudged white kitten with tabby bracelets in the same place, and streaked off back into the night.

"Let us hope that this will be the last," murmured Grandmother, thinking partly of the draught and partly of life in a small chalet with Dani and more than three kittens. But nobody else said anything at all because their eyes were fixed on the door. Dani's Klaus could do exactly what she liked and no question asked.

Back she came round the corner of the barn, but this time she walked slowly and majestically; her work was done. She carried in her mouth a pure white kitten, exactly like herself, gathered all three between her front paws, laid herself across Dani's chest, and started licking and purring as though her life depended on it.

"Shut the door, Lucien," said Grandmother, with a little sigh of relief—"and, Pierre, you had better find a basket for all those cats. The child will suffocate!"

Father chuckled—"In the morning, Mother," he replied. "Tonight they can stop where they are. The animal knows where they're welcome, and Dani won't mind."

Very gently he moved Klaus's right paw from Dani's chin; then he went off to lock up the cowshed.

Lucien rose to go. He went over to Grandmother and held out his hand.

"I must go," he said simply, "but thank you for letting me come in, and I hope Annette's foot will soon be better."

Grandmother, looking down into his face, held his hand for a moment in both hers. "Yes, you must go," she replied, "but remember, you are to come again. You will always be welcome."

Annette said nothing about waking Dani because Grandmother might have strongly disapproved, but after all a promise was a promise. She waited till Grandmother was washing up the chocolate cups and then she hopped to his side.

"Dani," she whispered, smoothing the damp hair back from his forehead. Dani sighed and flung his arms above his head but he did not wake.

"Dani!" said Annette, more loudly; and this time she pinched him. He opened his eyes, bright with sleep, and stared at her.

"Look, Dani," said Annette, "she's come—and she's brought you a present!"

Dani stared at the jumble of fur in his arms, too half-asleep to be astonished, and not quite sure whether he was dreaming or not.

"She's found three rats," he remarked.

"No, no, Dani," cried Annette. "Those aren't rats—they are three darling little kittens. She had them in the barn and now she's brought them to you. They're yours, Dani—a present from Klaus."

Dani blinked at them. "I knew she'd come," he murmured; "I asked God."

Annette knelt by the bed and gathered the whole bundle of Dani and Klaus and the kittens into her arms.

"And I asked the Lord Jesus to come in," she whispered. "And He did. That's two prayers answered in one night!"

But Dani did not hear; he had fallen asleep again with the tip of Klaus's tail in his mouth.

Chapter Sixteen

GRANDMOTHER's cold wet bandages were so successful that when Annette woke next morning the pain and swelling in her ankle were almost gone, although it still ached to walk on it. It had snowed in the night, too, and the drifts were so deep that Father had to dig a path to reach the cow-shed, so it was not a day to go out.

But Annette and Dani and Klaus and three kittens all underfoot in the living-room were just too much of a good thing, and by afternoon Grandmother suggested they should all go over to the hay barn and play there. So Dani carried his new family across in a basket and made nests for them in the hay, and turned somersaults, while Annette lay comfortably on her tummy and, with Grandmother's big Bible propped up in front of her, turned over the pages.

She wanted to find her own special verse about Jesus knocking at the door, which the minister had read, and she wanted to learn it by heart right through. She found it quite quickly because the Pastor had told them that it came in the last book in the Bible. Here it was, in Revelation, chapter 3, verse 20:

"Behold, I stand at the door, and knock: if any man hear My voice, and open the door, I will come in to him, and will sup with him, and he with Me."

Annette learned it so that she could say it without looking, and wondered what the last bit meant about having supper. She must remember to ask Grandmother when she next got a proper chance. Then she rested her head on her arms and just lay thinking for a time and watching Dani, who looked very queer doing somersaults because his good leg curled up and his bad leg stuck straight out.

She had opened the door to the Lord Jesus and He had come in and was living in her heart, and it had turned out as Grandmother had said. He had come in with His Spirit of forgiveness and love; the hard, angry thoughts had gone away like shadows before the light and it had suddenly not seemed difficult to forgive Lucien. In fact, she had stopped thinking very much about that bit of it, because when the Lord Jesus came in He had begun to show her how selfish and unloving and untruthful she had been herself, and what she was really worrying about now was whether Lucien would forgive her.

She had told him, and he had not seemed cross, but after all he had lost his prize, and Annette knew now that there was still something more she could do about it, if she really wanted to.

There were the Noah's ark animals. If she took them to the master and told him all about it he would see how beautifully Lucien could make things, and he would probably give Lucien another prize even now, if he really knew what had happened.

But she was so afraid of what the master would think and what the other children would say that she decided not to do any more about it. And directly she decided that, she found she did not want to think about her new text any more. It had stopped making her happy, and she began swinging on the beams instead, feeding the cows through a hole in the board until Father came over to milk, and then went down and sat in the manger and talked to him while he worked.

Darkness fell early, the children went in to their evening meal, and then it was Dani's bedtime. There was a commotion at bedtime because Grandmother wanted the kittens to sleep in the barn and Dani wanted them to sleep in the bed. In the end they each gave way a little, and the kittens slept under the bed; but there was a lot of conversation about it and by the time it was all over Grandmother felt tired out and sank into her chair with a little sigh. Annette drew her stool up beside her, but no sooner were they comfortably settled than there was a knock on the door, and Annette got up to open it.

Lucien stood in the doorway, twisting his hands together shyly, and Annette, although she wanted to be nice, felt shy too, and they stood there rather awkwardly waiting for each other to say something.

Grandmother looked up, surprised at the silence.

"Come in, Lucien," she called. "We are glad to see you. Annette, draw up another stool and sit down, both of you."

They sat down obediently, and Lucien, after saying that he had come to see how Annette's foot was, relapsed into silence. Annette, after saying it was "Much better, thank you," sat staring at the floor. Grandmother looked at them both very hard over the top of her spectacles.

"Annette and Lucien," said Grandmother suddenly, "you must stop this quarrel, and behave like sensible children. Lucien, you did a terrible thing, but you did not altogether mean to do it, and you have suffered for it. It's no good crying over spilt milk; now you must take courage and start again. Annette, you must learn to forgive and be kind and stop thinking yourself better than other people."

"I don't," said Annette rather surprisingly.

"You do," replied Grandmother, "or you would not find it so difficult to forgive them."

"But I have forgiven him," replied Annette. "Out on the mountain last night—and it wasn't very difficult to forgive, because I did something nasty to him as well, and when I told him about it, he said he'd forgive me too, didn't you, Lucien? So we're as bad as each other."

"Yes," replied Lucien simply. "But it wasn't such an awful thing as I did. I can make another horse, but I can't make Dani new legs. And, anyhow, everyone says you're good, and likes you; and nobody likes me."

"But perhaps," replied Annette, "it's because they all know what you did, and nobody knows what I did—and do you know, Lucien, this afternoon I was thinking I ought to tell the master, but somehow I don't think I should ever dare."

They were talking to each other; Grandmother sat listening, but because it was Grandmother they did not really mind. Now she spoke.

"Annette," she said suddenly, "how did you come to feel you could be forgiving? Two nights ago you told me you never could."

"Well, Grandmother, I opened the door, like you said, and then it all happened just like you said. When I asked Jesus to come in it somehow didn't seem so difficult."

"Yes," said Grandmother, "I knew it would be like that. But there is something else besides unkindness that the love of Jesus casts out. Fetch me my Bible, Annette."

Grandmother turned the pages slowly, peering at the print until she found the fourth chapter of the first Epistle of John, and pointed to verses 18 and 19.

"Read it, Annette," she said.

So Annette read aloud, slowly and distinctly:

" 'There is no fear in love; but perfect love casteth out fear; because fear hath torment. He that feareth is not made perfect in love. We love Him, because He first loved us.' "

"That's right," said Grandmother. "Perfect love casts out fear. When Jesus brings His perfect love into our hearts it drives out unkindness and selfishness, and it can also drive out fear. You see, if we really believe that He loves us perfectly there is nothing left to be afraid of. If He loves us perfectly He will never let anything really harm us."

Annette and Lucien sat thinking for a moment; then they smiled at each other, and Annette got up and went to her own cupboard and fetched out her Christmas bear and broke it in half as a peace-offering. They sat on their stools, Lucien munching happily, but Annette still thoughtful and troubled. She knew more clearly than ever now what was right, but still she didn't want to do it.

Lucien didn't stay very long, and when he was gone Annette said goodnight and rose to go to bed.

"Annette," said Grandmother, "remember that when Jesus comes in He only comes in as Master. You must do what He tells you, and not what you want any longer."

"Yes, Grandmother," said Annette rather sorrowfully. She went upstairs, and when she was undressed she knelt down to pray.

"Lord Jesus," she said, "I do want to do what You say. If I've really got to tell, please make me brave and stop me being afraid."

And she got into bed with a lighter heart and soon fell asleep. In the morning she woke early, and lay thinking until it was time to get up. Then, still limping a little, she dressed and went to the kitchen where Grandmother was stirring the coffee.

" Grandmother," she said firmly, " I want to go and see the the schoolmaster this morning."

" But what about your foot?" asked Grandmother.

" I'll go on the sledge."

" But how will you get back?"

" I don't know; I suppose I'll just limp back—but whatever happens, Grandmother, I must go and see the schoolmaster this very morning, and it can't wait."

" What's all this about?" chimed in Father, who was knocking the snow off his boots in the doorway. " If Annette wants to see the master she can come down with me. I'm taking the cheeses down to the train in the mule-cart. I'll drop Annette at the house, and pick her up on the way back from the station."

Annette's face brightened joyfully. She just couldn't have waited. If she waited another whole day she might start feeling terribly afraid again.

Sitting beside Father in the mule-cart, with the cheeses bumping about behind her, and the Noah's ark animals wrapped carefully in her hanky, she didn't feel quite so happy. She couldn't imagine what she would say to the master! What if he was very, very angry with her? He might easily be.

" What do you want to go to see the master for?" asked Father suddenly. " Are you tired of having no lessons to do?"

Annette leaned her golden head against his coat.

" No," she replied, shyly. " It's just something I want to tell him. It's a secret, Papa."

They jogged on in silence, until the white house came in sight. In summer it looked spotless, but against the purity of the snow it looked dingy and grey.

"Down you get," said Father, "and I'll be back for you in about half an hour."

The mule lurched on, and Annette, with her heart beating very fast, walked up the path, and stood for a long time without daring to knock. In fact, she might have stood there until it was time to go home again if the master had not seen her out of the window and come and opened the door without her knocking.

"Come in, come in," said the master genially, taking her into the little room where they had so often sat and done lessons together. He loved his children, and in holiday time he missed them and liked them to call on him. Annette went straight to the table and undid her handkerchief and arranged the little Noah's ark animals in a row.

"Lucien made them," she announced firmly. "Aren't they good!"

The master picked them up and examined them with interest. "They are beautifully done," he replied. "They are really exceptionally good for a boy of his age. He will soon be able to earn his living. I had no idea he could carve like that. Why did he not enter for the handwork competition?"

"He did," answered Annette, still very firmly. "That's what I came to tell you about. He made a little horse, and I smashed it when he wasn't looking because I was angry about Dani. But I'm sorry now, and I wondered if he couldn't have a prize after all—now that you know all about it."

The master looked at her thoughtfully. Her cheeks were scarlet and her eyes fixed on the ground.

"But I haven't another prize," said the schoolmaster at last. "There were only two. One was given to Pierre and one to you."

"Then Lucien ought to have the one that was given to Pierre. It was for the best boy, and Lucien's was much better than Pierre's."

"Oh, no," replied the master, "we couldn't do that. After all, Pierre won quite fairly. We couldn't take his prize away. If you really want him to have a prize you will have to give him yours. It was your fault that he lost it, wasn't it?"

"Yes," said Annette—and she sat in silence for full three minutes, thinking. Her prize was a beautiful book full of pictures of all the mountains in Switzerland. It lay in her drawer wrapped up in tissue paper and was her most precious possession.

Of course she could easily say no, and she knew the master would never force her to give it. But Grandmother had talked about perfect love. The Lord Jesus with His perfect love was living in her heart now, and He wouldn't want her to keep back anything.

"All right," said Annette at last.

"Good!" replied the schoolmaster, and there was a look of triumph in his eyes because in those three minutes he knew that Annette had won a very big battle. "You shall bring it to me when school begins, and I will present it to him in class, and the children shall see his carvings."

"Very well," said Annette—and she looked up timidly into his face to see if he thought her very, very wicked. But he only smiled down at her, and she went away knowing quite well that the old master loved her just as much as he had before.

Back up the hill with the empty mule-cart bumping and jolting over the snow; home again, and Annette climbed the steps and stood on the verandah, and Dani came and stood beside her with his arms full of kittens. Behind her Grandmother was cooking the dinner, and in front of her the sun had reached the valley.

She gazed down at the glistening roofs and the silver river, felt Dani's warm little hand in hers, and smelt the delicious smell of steaming soup behind her.

"This morning the valley was full of shadows," thought Annette to herself, "and now it's full of sunshine"—and she knew it was like the Lord Jesus coming into her heart and filling her with love and light and courage.

Chapter Seventeen

LUCIEN climbed the hill with a light step, and Annette walked by his side. They had never walked home from school together before, but now it was different.

It had been a very happy morning for Lucien. The master, without explaining why, had suddenly said that he had seen such a good piece of wood carving in the holidays that he had decided to award a further prize, and to everyone's astonishment Lucien had been called out to receive it, and Annette, who had expected the master to tell the whole story, had almost fainted with relief. Then all the children had gathered round to admire the little wooden animals, and freckle-faced Pierre had admired them louder than anyone else, remarking merrily that it was lucky for him they were given in so late or he would never have won the prize; to which everyone heartily agreed. Then they had all wanted to see his book, and the girls had cried out, "Why, it's just the same as Annette's book"—and Annette had waited uncomfortably for him to say, "It *is* Annette's book."

But he only replied, "Is it really?"—and when no one was looking he had winked at Annette.

When they were well out of sight of all the other children he held it out to her.

"It was nice getting a prize after all," he said, "but I don't want to keep it—truly I don't, Annette. It's your book, and I should hate to take it away from you."

Annette shook her head.

"No, you've got to keep it," she said. "Master said so; it's your book now."

"Well," said Lucien, "it really belongs to both of us so I think we'd better share it. Supposing I have it this month and you have it next month and me the next after that."

Annette brightened up. She wanted her book terribly.

"All right," she replied, "I'll do that if you like. On the first day of every month we'll change."

And so it became a custom that at five o'clock in the evening on the first of every month the possessor of the book would carry it solemnly to the neighbouring chalet and lay it on the table. This custom lasted all the year, and it was a good one, because each time they changed over they were reminded silently that real happiness comes from forgiving and sharing and helping one another.

"Let's sit down on this wood-pile and look at it," said Lucien, and they brushed the snow away from the logs and sat down and turned over the pages, for Lucien had never seen it before. He was keen on mountains and often studied the guide-books, and now he pointed out the different ways of ascent.

"That's the best way up the Matterhorn," he said eagerly, tracing out the path with his finger; "that's the way I shall climb it first"—and Annette, swinging her legs beside him, wished she were a boy, too, so that she could climb mountains.

They sat there a long time with the hot midday sun beating down on them, and the sky powder blue behind the white peaks. It was such fun looking at the picture that they forgot about being late for dinner, until a plaintive little voice quite close to them said,

"Annette, Granny said I could come and meet you—dinner's been ready a long time, and I've finished mine."

It was Dani, leaning heavily on his crutches, looking flushed and tired. Annette jumped guiltily off the wood-pile.

"Dani!" she cried, "you mustn't come so far down the mountain. You'll never get back. We must go home at once."

They started slowly up the road, but Dani was very tired. He had never been so far alone on his crutches before, but he had kept thinking that he would see his sister round the very next corner, and had hobbled on. In the end Lucien picked him up and carried him, and Annette carried the crutches.

Lucien carried him right to the door of the chalet, but nobody spoke. A sort of shadow seemed to have come between Lucien and Annette because both were thinking that however much they made up their quarrel Dani was still lame and nothing would give him back the full use of his legs.

"My leg aches so," said Dani rather peevishly as she carried him up the steps. "Put me on my bed, 'Nette."

So Annette laid him on the bed and gave him all his cats to play with, and she sat down and ate her bowl of cold potato soup. Father had gone back to his work, and Grandmother, after scolding her for being so late, went to the kitchen where Annette soon joined her. Grandmother was standing at the table skimming rich cream from bowls of milk, and Annette started to help her.

"What is the matter, Annette?" said Grandmother suddenly. "You look unhappy."

Annette didn't answer for a long time—then she said, "Grandmother."

"Yes, my child."

"Grandmother, you said that if I asked Jesus to come into my heart He would make me fond of Lucien, and send away the thoughts that didn't like him. And last week it was all right. But now when I see Dani with his leg hurting so, and remember he used to be so strong, all these thoughts come again."

"Yes," said Grandmother, "I expect they do. Every day of your life ugly, angry, selfish thoughts will knock at the door and try to get in again. Don't try and push them back yourself; ask the Lord Jesus to meet them with His love. Think about the love of Jesus all you can. Read about the love of Jesus every day in the Bible—and if you keep your heart full of it there just won't be room for those thoughts to stay."

"Where in the Bible, specially?" asked Annette.

"All through the Bible," answered Grandmother. "We have been reading the Gospel of Mark aloud at night lately, haven't we? and every page is full of the love of Jesus—His love to His disciples, His love to His enemies, His love to all poor and suffering people, His love for little children. Read carefully to yourself all the story of the life of Jesus and think a great deal about the way that He loved, and remember that it's that same love that came into your heart when you asked the Lord Jesus to come in."

"Yes," answered Annette rather absently—and to herself she thought, "I'll start today, and every morning when I wake up I'll read a story about how Jesus loved someone."

Lucien had gone home to his chalet, also thinking. The sight of Dani so tired made him sad. It was all very well for Annette—she had made up for the wrong things she had done, and had put it all right. But he could *never* make Dani's legs right.

Why had Annette forgiven him and been so different? he wondered, for about the hundredth time. At first he had thought it was just because he had found her in the snow, but now he knew it was more than that. She had talked about opening a door to Jesus, and Grandmother had said something about the love of Jesus turning out selfishness and unkindness.

The old man up the mountain had talked about mercy and forgiveness. Perhaps when you 'opened the door', whatever that meant, mercy and forgiveness came in as well as love. Perhaps it was all the same thing.

Anyhow, opening the door had made a very great difference to Annette. She used to be so stuck up and unforgiving—now she was quite humble and kind. It made Lucien think that Jesus Christ was not just Someone who lived long ago in the Bible stories, but Someone who could really do things now.

He had been walking slowly, but he had nearly reached the chalet. Twenty minutes before, when he and Annette had sat down on the woodpile, the sky had been blue and still, but now dark clouds were massing up behind the mountains, and a cold wind had begun to blow.

"It's blowing up for snow," said Lucien to himself. "There'll be a blizzard tonight."

The cattle were stamping restlessly in their stalls at the sound of the wind that had sprung up. Lucien went indoors quickly and joined his mother who was already eating her dinner.

"Come along," said his mother. "You're late. I'm glad you've no afternoon school because it's clouding over and I think we are in for a blizzard—what's that book you've got there?"

"It's a prize," replied Lucien. "The master gave it to me for carving. He saw something I did in the holidays."

"Well, that was nice of him," said his mother. "Did he know about the other one being smashed?"

"Yes," answered Lucien and changed the subject. He did not want to answer awkward questions. He was going to keep Annette's secret for her.

His thoughts kept going back to her as he sat in the

front room whittling away on a newspaper. His mother was ironing in the kitchen, so he was alone. "I asked Jesus to come in"—that was what Annette had said—and then Grandmother had read some verses out of the Bible . . . perhaps he could find them. He would like to read them again.

He went to the shelf and lifted down the dusty old family Bible with all the family births, marriages, and deaths written in front. His mother did not often read it, and he did not know very much about it, except what he had learnt at school. He could not remember where Grandmother's text had come, but he thought it was somewhere towards the end.

He could not find it, but he found other things. He found the Gospels and the stories he had heard at school of Jesus the Healer—how He had made blind men see, and lepers clean, and dead men live; yes, and there was a story about how He made someone walk!

'Arise, take up thy bed and walk.'

Well, if Jesus was really alive today, and had changed Annette's heart, surely He could make Dani walk, too.

Lucien had never really said his prayers since he was a tiny boy and had sometimes said them to his mother. But now he slipped across to the cow-shed, and ran up into the loft and knelt down in the very same spot where, those months before, he had lain and wept so bitterly.

He did not understand yet what it meant to open the door to Jesus, but he believed now that God was near and would listen when he prayed—and now he prayed with all his heart that God would heal Dani and make him walk properly again, as He cured people in the Bible.

He stayed there quite a long time and then slithered down and milked the cows. When he opened the door to cross with the buckets he was nearly thrown back by the snow driven almost horizontally by the wind. His mother was at the window looking out rather anxiously into the dusk.

"There's a real blizzard on," she said. "You'd better take the storm lantern and go to meet your sister; it's got dark so early."

But at that moment the door was flung open, and Marie, with the snow frozen on her hair and clinging to her coat, stood breathless and laughing in the doorway.

"It was a real fight with the wind getting up that slope," she panted, as she shook out her wet clothes and changed her boots. "I'm nearly worn out! Lucien, why didn't you come and meet me with the lantern? Mother, I hope supper's ready, because I'm famished."

They sat down at the table, Marie still chattering gaily with her cheeks as red as apples.

"What a day I've had!" she exclaimed. "People have been coming and going all day at the hotel—not that they'll get much winter sport this weather, poor things! I've been run off my feet; but I've had a good tip this evening. Look, Mother."

She pulled out a banknote and handed it to her mother. Madame Morel took it with pleased surprise. She, like her neighbours, had difficulty in making the little farm pay, and Marie was a good girl about bringing home her wages.

"Who gave you all that?" she enquired.

"Oh, such a nice gentleman!" cried Marie; "and I believe he's very famous, too. The proprietor's wife was telling me about him at dinner. He's a very clever doctor and he can cure almost anyone with broken bones. He's got a hospital down by the lake, and people go there from all over Switzerland and he cures them."

Lucien nearly choked in his excitement. He leaned across the table.

"Marie!" he burst out, "could he cure Dani Burnier?"

Marie stared at him in astonishment. She did not know that Lucien still troubled his head about little Dani Burnier.

"I don't know," she answered quite kindly. "They'd have to take him down to the lake if they wanted Monsieur Givet to see him. But they'd never have the money. Those clever men charge huge fees, Lucien, as much as all the Burnier cows put together, I should think."

Down to the lake! To Lucien, who had never left the valley, it seemed like the other end of the world.

He tried again.

"But, Marie, couldn't they take him to the hotel in the morning?"

"He's leaving on the early train—all his luggage was brought down tonight."

"But, Marie, couldn't they take him tonight?"

His earnestness touched Marie.

"Of course they couldn't, Lucien," she urged quietly. "Fancy taking a little child out in this blizzard! Any-how, the last train went hours ago, and the road over the Pass would be blocked on a night like this. It's quite impossible. Besides, I tell you they haven't the money! Stop worrying yourself about Dani Burnier, Lucien! You didn't mean to harm him really, and he's quite happy hopping about on that crutch, and getting thoroughly spoiled by that grandmother of his!"

Lucien said no more, and his sister went on to talk about the other visitors, and what the waitress had said to the porter, and what the proprietor had said to the cook. Lucien didn't hear a word. He had quite made up his mind what he was going to do, but there were three mighty difficulties in the way:

The doctor's fees were very high, and Lucien had no money.

His thoughts flew to the old man up the mountain. He had plenty of money if he could be persuaded to give it.

The Pass was probably blocked.

Well, he could try. If he failed, he would know at least that he had done his best.

Would the doctor come? Would he leave the train that would carry him to his important hospital by the lake, and take a local train with a boy he didn't know, and climb the mountain in a blizzard to see a peasant child?

It was all most unlikely, but there was just a chance that he would. Marie had called him a nice gentleman.

"I've finished my supper, Mother," said Lucien. "I'm going upstairs."

Chapter Eighteen

ONCE in his room Lucien moved with great speed. There wasn't a minute to be lost.

He unhitched his cloak from the cupboard and put on his woolly balaclava helmet that covered his ears. Then he wound his puttees round his legs and put on his stoutest boots. Then he wrote a note to his mother telling her he would not be back till morning.

He tiptoed down the stairs into the kitchen, and filled his pockets with bread and cheese and a box of matches. Then he silently lifted the latch of the back door and crept across to the barn. The storm lantern hung on the wall, and Lucien lit it and was comforted by its steady ray. He wondered whether to take his skis, but decided it was too dark. He opened the far door of the barn and stepped out into the windy snow meadows, and the blizzard nearly buffeted him over. He was safely away. His great adventure had begun.

If the wind was like this in the field, he wondered what it would be like on the Pass. Surely he would be blown over and buried in the drifts! Well, he would see when he got there. In the meanwhile he must think hard about reaching the old man.

It was a relief to reach the woods. Here, although the trees shuddered and tossed their branches and made eerie noises, he himself was sheltered, and the snow on the path was less deep than the snow in the meadows. He could move more quickly without floundering.

Up and on through the tossing trees, until he could see a comforting orange glow of light in the old man's window. The end of the first stage of his journey was in sight. He braced himself to meet the wind as he came out in the open again, struggled to the old man's door and knocked.

"Who's there?" said the old man very cautiously from within.

"Me, Lucien."

The door was flung open instantly, and the old man drew him in.

"Lucien, my boy," he cried, peering at him in astonishment, "whatever brings you here, in this weather, at this time of night? What has happened?"

Lucien, after his battle with the wind, sank down on the bench for a moment to regain his breath. He did not like asking the old man for his money, but nothing must stand in the way of his quest.

"You once said," began Lucien, looking up into the old man's face, his eyes bright with anxiety, "that you had a lot of money to give to someone if they really needed it. I've found someone who really needs it. If you will give me your money I think little Dani Burnier's leg might be made better."

"How could that be?" asked the old man, looking very attentively at the boy.

"There's a doctor at the hotel where my sister works," explained Lucien, "who can cure lame people and heal broken bones. I'm going now to ask him to come and see Dani; but my sister says he would want a lot of money."

"You're going now?" repeated the old man, "in this weather? You must be mad, boy! you could never cross the Pass in this weather."

"I think I could!" replied Lucien doggedly. "The blizzard started only a few hours ago, and the fresh snow won't be deep yet, if I hurry—but it's no good going unless I've got the money!"

The old man did not answer for a minute. He seemed to be struggling with himself.

"I would give it if I was sure of the man," he said doubtfully. "But I don't want to waste or lose it. How do I know that he is an honest man? What is his name, Lucien?"

"His name is M. Givet. My sister says he's a famous man."

"Monsieur Givet!"

The old man repeated the words softly in a strange voice, as though he thought he must have made a mistake about them. It seemed to Lucien that he had turned rather pale. But without another word he turned away, took a key from one of his own carved boxes, and opened a little cupboard in the wall behind his bed. From this he drew out an old sock stuffed with notes.

"Take it all," he said, "and give it all to Monsieur Givet. Tell him it is all his if he will cure the child. Tell him . . . tell him, Lucien, that it is the payment of a debt."

His voice shook a little, and Lucien glanced at him in surprise, but he was too glad to wonder much. He had never seen so much money before in his life. He put the whole bundle inside his shirt, buttoned his coat and cloak over it, and made for the door.

"Thank you very, very much," he said hastily at the door. "I'll come and tell you what happens."

The old man came to the door to watch him go, and held his lantern high to light the path. Lucien had gone only a few steps when the old man called to him loudly above the wind.

"Lucien!"

Lucien ran back.

"Yes, Monsieur."

"You won't forget the message, will you?"

"No," replied Lucien carefully. "I'm to say it's the payment of a debt. I won't forget. Good-bye, Monsieur."

He was making off again into the night when the old man called again.

"Lucien."

The boy ran back, impatient at the delay.

"Yes, Monsieur?"

"You won't tell him anything about me, will you? Don't tell him my name, will you, Lucien?"

"I don't know your name," Lucien reminded him.

"And don't you tell him where I live, Lucien!"

"No, Monsieur," Lucien answered him, too impatient to wonder; "I'll just say it's the payment of a debt. Good-bye, Monsieur."

He sped off as fast as he could through the deep soft snow, afraid that the old man might call him again. At the margin of the wood he turned and waved his lantern. Through the whirling snow he could still see the dim figure of the old man black against the light of his open door.

He must be very quick—the snow was still falling—very soon the Pass would be uncrossable, if it were not so already.

He thought it probably would be uncrossable already on foot. He would go into the cowshed on the way down and get his skis.

He stumbled his way over the last field, sinking in at every step. The cowshed was mercifully still unlocked and Lucien stepped in with extreme caution. He had just lifted down his skis when the further door was flung open and his mother and Marie came in, waving a lantern. Lucien propped his skis against the wall and fell flat on his face on the dirty floor behind the largest cow.

"He's not here," said his mother, flashing her lantern round the shed, her voice sharp with anxiety. "I believe you're right, Marie, he's got some mad notion about getting to that doctor. He'll be floundering along that mountain road by now, and the stupid boy hasn't even taken his skis. I wonder whether we could persuade Monsieur Burnier to go after him and fetch him back—he can't have got far on foot."

"I think we'd better," agreed Marie, and her voice sounded agitated, too. "Monsieur Burnier will easily catch him up on skis and stop him before he gets anywhere really dangerous. Let's go now and ask him."

They went off hastily, and Lucien, pressed against the cow's flanks, jumped to his feet. There wasn't a moment to lose.

It would take them two or three minutes to get on their mackintoshes and boots. In this weather it would take them a quarter of an hour to reach the Burniers' chalet. Another ten minutes while they told their story and while Monsieur Burnier collected his lantern and boots and skis. He had roughly about half an hour's start—it ought to be all right, but then he was only a light child and Monsieur Burnier a heavy, skilful man who could ski much faster than Lucien.

Very, very carefully, he crept from the shed, relit his lantern which he had blown out when he heard the latch move, and fastened his skis. Stemming carefully, he started off, holding the lantern out in front of him, his head well down because the blizzard was blinding.

Down over the meadows and once again he reached the friendly shelter of the forest path where he could look in front of him. Out across the low fields skirting the village, and here the wind was less furious and Lucien could look straight ahead and go faster.

He crossed the silent market square with its frozen fountain and glided on downhill past the village dairy, past the station and over the bridge that led across the river, and then he paused for a few minutes to get his breath; for he had reached the very lowest part of the valley, and now he must start climbing the other side right up over the Pass that ran between two mountains.

He glanced back fearfully in case Monsieur Burnier should be following, but there was no one in sight. He suddenly felt terribly lonely, and longed for the village with its dark chalets and warm orange windows. For a moment he almost wished Monsieur Burnier would catch him up; but he pushed away the thought and began his climb.

The snow on the valley road was not too bad. Lucien shouldered his skis and found he could walk without very much difficulty. He could still hear the wind howling in the woods above him, but the blizzard seemed to be stopping.

Once again he plunged into the woods and climbed, weary and afraid. These were not the familiar woods of his own side of the mountain, but dark strange woods.

He climbed through the woods for three hours, his mind full of fears and horrors. Every story he had ever heard about the perils of the mountains crowded into his mind—avalanches, treacherous drifts, breaking boughs. He thought of the St. Bernard dogs trained to rescue foundered travellers. Well, there were no dogs round here. He supposed he would just founder.

Unless, of course, he chose to go back.

He stopped for a moment wondering that the thought had not occurred to him before. How simple to buckle on his skis and stem carefully down the zig-zagging forest path and go home?

"I did my best," he would tell them, "but I couldn't get through"—and the Burniers would no doubt think it very heroic of him even to have tried.

The wind was roaring horribly and the great trees crying aloud and tossing their arms; he was nearly at the top of the forest now, out on the wild wastes of the Pass where the wind might pick him up and whirl him over the rocks like a snowflake. He found his teeth were chattering and he was crying.

"I'm so frightened," he sobbed to himself. "I can't go on. I know I'll be killed on the Pass. I wish Monsieur Burnier would come."

And then as he stooped to buckle his skis he suddenly remembered that warm, sheltered moment, when he and Annette and Grandmother had sat round the stove together and Grandmother had talked about being afraid.

"Perfect love casteth out fear . . . if we really believe that Jesus loves us perfectly there is nothing left to be afraid of . . . if He loves us perfectly He will never let anything really harm us."

Lucien paused, with his hands on the buckles, arrested by his thoughts. So he was not alone after all. Grandmother had said that Jesus loved him perfectly, and if He loved perfectly He would not leave a child alone in darkness and danger. It was just as though Someone stronger than the night, the wind, the terror, and the darkness had suddenly come to him and taken his hand and pointed up the hill.

He shouldered his skis and went on.

"Perfect love casteth out fear," he murmured to himself over and over again. It was true, too. He had stopped feeling so terribly frightened because he had stopped feeling alone.

He had reached the top of the forest and come out into the open, and now he could think of nothing at all except of how to go on.

Mercifully, it had stopped snowing and the sky was less inky. Now and again a pale moon broke through the ragged mass of hurrying clouds, and at such moments, if he lifted his face for an instant, he could see rocks rising to his side, and knew that if he just went on straight in front of him he must reach the top sometime.

And then, after what seemed a very long time, he was struck by a blast that sent him reeling backwards, and he lay gasping in the snow.

"I shall never be able to get up again," said Lucien to himself, almost too exhausted to care whether he ever got up again or not. And then once again he remembered about that perfect love, and because he was a child, and because he felt the Saviour so close beside him, instead of praying, he just held out his hands to be lifted.

And after a moment or two a little strength seemed to come back to him and he struggled to his feet again, and found that the ground in front of him sloped gently downwards. He had crossed the Pass.

Now he became thankful for the wind, because his legs were too weary and numb to steer his skis, and without that gale sweeping up the Pass against him he would have gone dangerously fast. As it was, he travelled slowly, crouching for a little way, and then his legs crumpled up altogether and he sat down and let the skis carry him like a toboggan.

He was so cold that he had stopped feeling cold; sitting there, sliding effortlessly down the hill, he wondered if he were going to sleep. A sort of drowsy numbness seemed to be stealing over him, until suddenly he felt a jerk, and, coming to, he realized that the wind was no longer buffeting him and his skis had stuck in a drift.

He gave himself a shake and looked round. He had reached the forest again, and that was why the wind had dropped. He could not remember anything of the last few minutes—but apparently the Lord in His perfect love had guided him, for the smooth forest track lay at his feet, winding away through the trees, and he had not missed his way.

He roused himself, for it was very dark and the storm lantern only gave light a few feet ahead. He must steer himself carefully because the path zigzagged and he might fall over the edge or run into the tree-trunks. But he was sheltered from the wind which had beaten the sense and feeling out of him; and that, for the moment, was all he cared about. He was beginning to feel that his limbs belonged to him again, and very painful they were!

Down—down—down—the forest was almost quiet now, for he was travelling towards a deep valley. Sometimes he stood, sometimes he sat; and towards early morning the clouds dispersed, and the moon shone out and its light pierced the boughs. When at last he glided out into the open the fields lay still and silver, and the dark town was below him. In half an hour's time he would be there, knocking on the door of the great hotel, and then. . . .

"If Jesus really loves me perfectly," thought Lucien, "He can't have let me come all this way for nothing"—and too weary to think any more, he struck out across the meadows.

Chapter Nineteen

MONSIEUR GIVET woke very early, and the first thing he thought of was that the storm had stopped, and the valley was still. The second thing he remembered was that he was going home today.

He got out of bed and dressed, and whistled while he shaved. Just as he was finishing there was a knock on the door.

"Come in," called Monsieur Givet, surprised, for it was much too soon for the early breakfast he had ordered. It was only about half-past five.

The door opened, and the night porter came in; he looked as though he had some rather mysterious news to impart.

"Excuse me, sir," he began, holding his head enquiringly on one side, "but I suppose you weren't by any chance expecting a visitor."

"A visitor?" echoed Monsieur Givet, still more surprised, "at this hour and in this weather? I certainly am not."

"Well, sir," said the porter warming up to his story, "it's like this. Just a quarter of an hour ago I heard a little rap on the door and when I opened it there on the step stands a boy on skis, about twelve years old, sir, white as a sheet and looking more like a ghost than a boy. 'I want Monsieur Givet,' said he without so much as a good morning, and down he sits on the step and leans his head against the doorway. 'Well,' I says to him, 'you can't come calling on people at this hour of the morning, laddie —he's asleep in his bed.' 'I'll wait, then,' says he, and his head sinks down on to his knees.

"Well, I don't like to see a child taken like that so I took off his skis and dragged him in and sat him in a chair. 'Where have you come from?' I asked him. 'From Pré d'Oré,' says he. 'How's that?' says I. 'The early train isn't in yet.'

"'I came over the Pass,' says he—and, Monsieur, the more I look at that boy the more I feel like believing him. He's sitting down in the hall now, and when I passed your door, sir, and saw the light on I thought I'd come in and ask if you'd like to see him."

"I'll come and see him, certainly," answered Monsieur Givet, "but I can't quite swallow that story that he's just come over the Pass. I don't believe the guides themselves could have crossed last night. It must have been terrible up there."

The porter shrugged his shoulders, and led the way downstairs; but when they reached the hall they both ran forward together with a little cry of dismay.

Lucien had slithered off the chair and lay in a dead faint on the floor; his face looked strangely white.

Monsieur Givet picked the unconscious child up in his arms. "I'll take this boy to my room," he said to the alarmed porter; "you bring me some hot water bottles and some brandy and some hot coffee, and be as quick as you can."

Upstairs in his room he laid the boy on his bed, removed his sodden boots and socks, and chafed his numb feet. Then he drew off the snow-crusted clothes and wrapped him in blankets; by this time the night porter had arrived, puffing very hard, with the bottles and the brandy and the steaming coffee.

Monsieur Givet arranged the bottles and held a teaspoonful of brandy to Lucien's white lips. Lucien did not open his eyes, but he gave a tired sigh and swallowed the brandy.

"That's right, laddie," said Monsieur Givet. "You'll soon be round."

When Lucien opened his eyes a few minutes later he looked straight up into a kind, brown face, and couldn't think where he was. He felt deliciously warm and comfortable and drowsy and thought he would never want to move again as long as he lived—but he would like to know who the man with the kind, brown face was, who looked at him so intently.

"Who are you?" he murmured.

Monsieur Givet didn't answer at once. He raised Lucien's head and fed him with hot coffee, and Lucien swallowed very slowly because it seemed too much of an effort to swallow just at the moment. When he had finished he said again,

"Who are you, and where am I?"

"I'm Monsieur Givet," replied the doctor. "I don't know you, but I understand that you wanted me."

Lucien stared at him rather stupidly; he had been so tired that he had almost forgotten what he had come for; but with the warmth and the food things were beginning to get clear again, and at last he spoke.

"Are you a great, clever, famous doctor?"

"No; I'm just a doctor."

"But can you make lame children walk?"

"It depends why they are lame. Sometimes I can."

"He's lame because he fell over a precipice. He walks with a crutch and a big boot."

"Who does?" asked the bewildered Monsieur Givet.

"Little Dani Burnier; he's six. He lives in the chalet next to mine. So I came to ask if you could make him well. I've got enough money to pay you."

"But how did you hear of me?"

"My sister told me about you last night. My sister's a maid here."

"But how did you get here in that storm?"

"I came over the Pass on my skis."

"You can't have done, not in that blizzard."

"But I did; there's no other way to come."

It was quite true; there was not. Monsieur Givet sat looking at the boy as though he were some rare curiosity and, as the doctor stared, Lucien's hand stole under the shirt he was still wearing and drew out the fat stocking.

"Please, sir," he said, "would this be enough to make him better?"

Monsieur Givet drew out the contents of the old sock, and gave an exclamation of astonishment.

"Boy," said Monsieur Givet quite gently but very firmly, "before we go any further you must tell me where you got all this money from. Do you know how much there is?"

"No," said Lucien rather drowsily. "But my sister said you'd want a lot. Is it enough?"

"It's far too much," replied the doctor. "But where did you get it from?"

"An old man I'm friends with gave it me," murmured Lucien, who felt he could not keep his eyes open another minute, "and there was a message. He said it was the payment of a debt—and you were to take it all."

"Who was this old man?" asked Monsieur Givet. "Just

tell me that, and then you shall go to sleep. What was his name?"

"Please, sir, I don't know."

"Where does he live?"

"Please, he made me promise not to tell you"—and with that his eyes closed and his head rolled over on one side. Lucien was fast asleep.

Monsieur Givet was in rather an awkward situation. His train was due to leave in three-quarters of an hour. But the boy lying on the bed had risked his life to come to him. It might be all for nothing, but he couldn't disappoint such determined courage by refusing to see the little cripple; and yet Lucien would probably sleep for hours now.

He left the room softly, went downstairs to the telephone, and rang up his wife.

"Are you there, Marthe?" he began. "Darling, I'm so sorry, but I shan't be home till late tonight—such a strange thing has happened . . ." and into her sympathetic ears he poured the whole mysterious story.

As he left the office he was nearly knocked over by a girl—a red-eyed, pale-faced girl, in outdoor clothes. She caught his hand.

"Oh, sir," she cried, "Porter tells me you've got my little brother safe upstairs. Oh, sir, Mother and I thought he was dead in the drifts. Oh, sir, I must go home quick and tell my mother he's here."

Monsieur Givet sat down beside her on a sofa and tried to get some sort of an explanation out of her, but she could talk of little but the terrible night she and her mother had passed through. Monsieur Burnier had been out all night looking for him, but as they had told him that Lucien had gone on foot he had spent his time searching the edge of the woods. It would have been quite impossible for a child on foot to have come out into the deep snow meadows of the Pass, and the wind and blizzard had covered his solitary ski-tracks. On the wood path Monsieur Burnier had found footprints, but they had not gone beyond the margin of the forest, and Monsieur Burnier had searched the drifts in vain; he had come home with his sad news in the early hours of the morning.

Marie could tell Monsieur Givet very little about Dani. She was too upset to work, and now that she knew Lucien was safe she was in a hurry to take him home. She would telephone the Post Office now and they would get a child to run up the mountain with the news so that her mother would hear more quickly.

But Monsieur Givet would not hear of Lucien going home just yet. Marie would go home by herself and when Lucien woke he would bring him on the train. Marie had better get someone to send a mule sleigh to the station as Lucien would probably be too stiff to walk.

Marie agreed to everything, and made off as fast as she could go while Monsieur Givet went back to his room. Lucien still lay just as he had left him with his cheek resting on his hand, but there was a faint tinge of colour in his face—he looked much better. Monsieur Givet sat down and watched him, and wondered again how the boy had come into the possession of such an enormous sum of money. Who was the old man who had sent such a strange message?

"The payment of a debt!"—Monsieur Givet decided to look into the matter very closely.

Lucien woke at midday, and once again could not remember where he was for quite a long time. He was aching in every joint, but it was a warm pleasant ache, provided no one wanted him to move. Monsieur Givet heard a little movement and came to see what was happening.

"Well?" he asked kindly, "how do you feel?"

"All right, thank you," answered Lucien; and then he remembered that he'd been to sleep, and added anxiously, "Will you have time to see the little boy I told you about, sir?"

"Yes," said Monsieur Givet sitting down beside him, "we'll go after dinner. I'll ring now for them to send up dinner for two, and while we eat you can tell me all about this little boy, and all about this old man who you say sent the money."

"I can't tell you about the old man, sir," replied Lucien, "because I promised not to. He's a sort of secret, and no one ever goes to see him except me. He said I was just to tell you that it was the payment of a debt and nothing else at all, sir—and he's been so kind to me, I couldn't break my promise."

"All right," said Monsieur Givet. "You shan't break your promise; I won't ask you anything more about him. Tell me about this little cripple—when did he hurt himself, and how did it happen?"

The doctor noticed that Lucien went very red. He didn't answer for a few minutes. He didn't want to tell his new friend what had really happened, but as Monsieur Givet would be sure to find out from the Burniers it might be better if he heard it first from Lucien. So he replied,

"It was my fault, really. It was last spring. I was teasing him. I pretended to drop his kitten over the ravine, then by mistake I really did drop it—and Dani tried to rescue it, fell into the stream and hurt his leg and since then he's never walked properly—only with crutches—and I thought perhaps . . ."

His lips trembled and his voice trailed off miserably into a whisper. But he had said enough. For the doctor loved and understood children and in those few broken sentences he had grasped the whole story, and he knew that this tired boy lying on the bed had been punished very bitterly.

"Lucien," he said, "we'll see this child together. It may be that God is going to make you the means of curing him. You know, Lucien, you have a great deal to thank God for; I think He must have been looking after you in a very special way last night or you would never have come across the Pass alive."

"Yes, I know," answered Lucien shyly and eagerly. "You see, only yesterday I prayed that God would make Dani better—and then when I heard about you I thought it was the answer—but when I got to the forest I felt frightened and nearly went back—but I remembered something I heard at Christmas and thought I'd go on instead."

"What did you remember?" asked Monsieur Givet, gently.

"I remembered a text in the Bible Dani's grandmother read to us," answered Lucien slowly. "I can't remember it all—but it said that perfect love casts out fear—and Grandmother said Jesus' love was perfect—and so I wasn't afraid and I went on, and I can't remember much about the top—but I got down safely."

"Yes," replied Monsieur Givet; "I don't think anything but the perfect love of the Lord Jesus could have sheltered you in that storm, or guided you on the right road, or kept you from being too afraid to go on. He's been very, very good to you, Lucien. Let's thank Him now, before our dinner comes."

So Lucien buried his face in the pillow and Monsieur Givet knelt by the bed and prayed. He thanked the Saviour for His perfect love that is stronger than storm or tempest, which had guided Lucien's steps through the darkness and saved him from fear and death; then he prayed for little Dani, that God would give him, the doctor, skill to heal that lame leg.

Lucien, with his face in the pillow, prayed as well, only not aloud, "Lord Jesus," he cried in his heart, "You were so near me on that mountain and I wasn't afraid. Don't go away again; I want to open my door like Annette did. Please come in."

Chapter Twenty

MONSIEUR BURNIER met the train himself, with his own mule-sleigh, and drove Monsieur Givet and Lucien up to the chalet. All the villagers came to their front doors to see the doctor pass, as everyone had heard the story, and Monsieur Givet had grown in fame and magnificence every time it was repeated; while the children almost expected him to carry a magic wand, at a touch of which Dani Burnier would be immediately healed. Lucien was spoken of as though he were some modern miracle, but he could not hear what everyone was saying because the mule was trotting fast and the bells were jangling loudly —and that was a very good thing, for it would have been a pity to make him vain.

He sat on the sleigh, propped up against Monsieur Givet. He could not have walked a step if he had tried, and had to be lifted from the train; his limbs were so stiff that they refused to function at all. But in spite of his weariness he felt well and happy and full of hope, and his heart seemed to be chiming as merrily as the mule-bells as they neared the chalet.

Monsieur Burnier sat silent in the driver's seat, not knowing what to make of it all. It was rather a responsibility having such a famous man on that sleigh. He only hoped that the mule, who was very frisky that day, wouldn't tip the sleigh over the edge on one of the corners

—an event which happened fairly frequently, for the sleigh was very big and the path very narrow.

He was worried about the money, too; of course he would give every penny he possessed to see Dani cured, but he didn't possess very many pennies and what if they weren't enough? Perhaps this very famous man would accept a young bull by way of payment.

Fortunately they reached the chalet without any adventures or upsets, and Monsieur Burnier helped the doctor to alight, and then lifted poor Lucien in his strong arms and carried him up the steps into the front room, where he laid him on the couch. He, too, was pleased to see Lucien, for he had spent a weary, anxious night searching for him in the drifts.

Grandmother, Annette, and Dani looked rather odd, as though they were about to have their photograph taken. They were all dressed in their very best, sitting in a stiff little group on the edge of the best chairs. They looked as though they had been sitting there expecting the very famous man for a long time. When he entered Annette and Dani looked at Grandmother and rose gravely to their feet; Grandmother on account of her rheumatics merely bowed her head.

Dani was not at all pleased. He had thought that a very famous man would be dressed in a red robe like the over-lord who made William Tell shoot the apple, in Annette's Swiss history book. He thought he would have a splendid curling yellow beard, too, and probably ride a white battle-horse; while this stranger who came in behind Father was too ordinary for words. Dani felt very cross and stuck out his bottom lip and scowled.

The doctor sat down on a chair as far away as possible from the group and smiled at them. He had a nice broad smile, and Dani forgot his disappointment and smiled back.

Monsieur Givet put his hand in his pocket, withdrew a caramel and held it out.

"Do you want a caramel, Dani?" he asked.

Dani grinned happily and nodded his yellow head hard; a caramel was much better than a scarlet robe and a battle-horse.

"Come and fetch it, then," said Monsieur Givet, and Dani hopped delightedly across the room; while he hopped the doctor watched him with the closest attention. When the child reached him he lifted him on to his knee and put the caramel into his mouth.

He liked this family immensely. He liked Grandmother, who leaned forward and watched him so shrewdly, as much as to say, "That child is mine—be careful what you do to him, or you will have me to reckon with!" He liked Father, with his honest brown face and his shoulders bowed with labour. He liked Annette, with her corn-coloured plaits and her spotless striped pinafore—and most of all he liked the chuckling, friendly, blue-eyed little person who sat noisily sucking a caramel on his lap. He noticed too that there was no mother, and wondered whether it was the old woman or the little girl who kept the chalet in such perfect order.

"Does your leg hurt you?" asked Monsieur Givet.

"No," answered Dani.

"No, Monsieur," corrected Grandmother.

"Monsieur," added Dani, who was always obliging; "only sometimes, when I walk without my crutches—my crutches have got bears' heads on them; would you like to see them?"

"Very much indeed," said Monsieur Givet, and as Dani hopped over to fetch them he again watched him with the closest attention.

"I can do 'normous great hops on my crutches," announced Dani, who was not modest. "Would you like to see me do a 'normous great hop?"

"Yes, please, I should," answered the doctor.

"Be careful of the chairs, Dani," chimed in Grandmother, who had forbidden Dani to do enormous great hops in the house, and Annette hastily cleared away two kittens, for there was no knowing where Dani might land.

The hop was a huge success, and the doctor clapped his hands. "Well done," he cried; "that was exactly like a kangaroo I once saw at the Zoo. Now put down your crutches and walk to me without them."

Dani limped towards him, smiling, but dragging his lame leg rather pitifully. Monsieur Givet smiled back, lifted the little boy very gently on to his knee again and gave him another caramel.

And only then did Grandmother, who had been watching very closely, turn to Annette.

"Annette," she said, "put the kettle on and make a pot of afternoon tea and bring out the bricelet biscuit tin." Grandmother did not believe in pandering to the great until she was sure they really deserved it.

While Annette was getting tea, Monsieur Givet laid Dani flat on the table, and twisted and turned his leg about for a very long time—in fact, when he had finished the tea was ready and Grandmother invited him to sit down and drink with them; he sat down and seemed lost in thought.

"Well," said Grandmother at last, rather sharply. "Can you do anything for him?"

Every eye in the room was fixed on him as they waited for his answer—except Dani, whose eyes were fixed on the bricelet biscuits, because they had forgotten to pass him one and Grandmother would be cross if he got up and helped himself. Bricelet biscuits are delicious—they are thin and crisp and golden—and Grandmother made them once a month in a special grill.

Monsieur Givet did not answer at once; he turned to Dani instead.

"Dani," he said, "would you like to be able to run about like other little boys?"

Dani hesitated. He was not quite sure; he was the only boy in the village who possessed bear crutches, and it made him a very special and distinguished person. Then he remembered that spring was coming, and unless he could run about he would not be able to chase the baby goats in the meadows as he had done last year—and chasing baby goats was such fun that perhaps it was worth while being ordinary.

So he said, "Yes, thank you, I would; and please, Grandmother, may I have a bricelet biscuit?"

But no one answered. Lucien and Annette were sitting with their cups poised in mid-air and both were rather pale. Everyone was still staring at Monsieur Givet.

"Dani," said the doctor suddenly, "where's that fine cat gone?"

"To the wood-shed," said Dani. "Would you like to see her? She's got three kittens, too."

"Yes, please," answered Monsieur Givet, and Dani limped off to find Klaus—and as he passed the table he helped himself to two bricelet biscuits, and nobody even seemed to notice.

As soon as the door had closed on Dani, Monsieur Givet turned to Father.

"I think I may be able to help you," he said, leaning forward and speaking very earnestly, "although I can't tell for certain until I've seen an X-ray of it. I think the bone was never properly set and has joined up wrongly, and that I could break it again and pull it out straight. But it would mean an operation and a long stay in hospital. Would you be willing to let him come?"

Father rubbed his hands together miserably and looked helplessly—first at Grandmother and then at Annette. Operations had never come Father's way and the word sounded horrible. Besides he had been told that operations were very expensive, and he wouldn't be able to pay.

"How much would it cost?" he asked at last, scratching his head.

"It wouldn't cost you anything," replied Monsieur Givet. "Lucien has paid for it himself, in any case. I can't explain now because your little boy will be back and we must decide before he comes. Will you let me take him?"

"Yes," replied Grandmother, who hadn't been asked.

"When?" enquired Annette.

"Tomorrow morning," replied Monsieur Givet. "I shall be catching the early train, and I'll take Dani with me."

"Where am I going in the train?" said a clear voice. Dani had come in quietly through the back door and no one had noticed him. Now he stood at Monsieur Givet's elbow with his arms full of kittens, looking pleased. He had only once been in a train in his life—just for ten minutes—but he had never forgotten it.

No one answered. They were still staring at Monsieur Givet.

"Where, Grandmother?" enquired Dani again.

The doctor turned to Dani.

"Dani," he said, "you're coming with me down to the lake, and you're going to stay with me for a little and I hope I'm going to make your leg better. Will you like that?"

Dani looked suspicious.

"And Annette?" he said firmly. "And Grandmother and Papa and Klaus and the kittens? Yes, Monsieur, we shall all like it very much."

"Oh, no, Dani," cried Annette. "We can't all come too; you've got to be good and go by yourself. Monsieur will look after you and you'll soon come back"—but she was nearly crying herself.

The effect of these words was terrible. Dani flung himself, kittens and all, into Annette's arms and burst into the most deafening roars of rage and despair.

Never had the Burniers heard such a noise. Annette hugged and kissed his top half—Grandmother shook and jostled his lower half, Father pressed handfuls of bricelet biscuits into his clenched fists; but nothing helped. The family looked at each other helplessly. Monsieur Givet knew that, unless he could think of something very quickly, he would lose the day.

He turned to Grandmother.

"Does the little girl know anything about looking after children?" he shouted above the din.

"She brought up this one," shouted back Grandmother; which did not seem to Monsieur Givet a very good testimonial just at that moment.

"You had better send her with her little brother then," yelled Monsieur Givet. "She can help my wife."

"Dani," screamed Annette, shaking him hard to make him listen, "I'm coming, too!"

Dani stopped instantly, gave three hiccups and smiled. Monsieur Givet did not smile back. He picked up the little boy and spoke to him gravely.

"I'm afraid you are very spoiled, Dani," he said. "When you come to my hospital you will have to do what you are told without any fuss or screaming."

Dani pommelled him joyfully on the chest.

"And Annette!" he replied, and smiled again. He knew he had come out top this time.

Monsieur Givet put Dani down. "I am going to take Lucien home, if you can lend me a sledge," he said. "So I will say good-bye for the present. The two children will meet me on the platform at 8.30 tomorrow morning with all that they need for the next two or three months. Annette shall help my wife in the morning, and attend evening classes for her schooling. In the afternoons she can be free to be with her little brother."

Father shook hands dumbly and wiped his brow. Events were moving so fast that he felt he had been left right behind. But he was just beginning to understand that for two months, starting tomorrow, he had got to live without Annette and Dani, in a silent, tidy chalet; and the desolation of that thought blotted out everything else. He went stumbling over to the cowshed to milk and to try to think things out with his bewildered head pressed against Paquerette's kind, warm flanks.

Grandmother said good-bye at the door, and held the doctor's hand for some moments in her own. "You are a good man," she said suddenly. "God will reward you."

Monsieur Givet pulled Lucien to his own chalet on a borrowed sledge, and carried him in to his mother. She pretended to be very angry with him.

"You naughty boy, Lucien," she cried, "going off like that and giving us all such a dreadful fright—how could you do such a thing? You deserve a beating . . ."—but she took him almost roughly from Monsieur Givet's arms, helped him up the stairs, and put him to bed herself.

Then she came back, sat down at the table, flung her black apron over her face and began to cry.

"You have a very brave son, Madame," said Monsieur Givet.

"He's a very naughty boy," snapped Madame, and because she was so terribly proud of him and so glad to see him safe she began to cry again worse than before.

She and Marie had been baking a big batch of Lucien's favourite cakes all the morning, and the house was full of the good smell. They invited Monsieur Givet to sit down and eat with them, but he refused because he still had something important to do and time was getting on.

"I believe," he began, rather abruptly, "that Lucien knows some old man round here—can you tell me where he lives?"

"An old man?" repeated Marie. "Oh, yes, that would be that old man up the mountain that teaches Lucien wood-carving. They spend hours together, although what Lucien sees in him, goodness knows! Most people say he's crazy."

"Can you tell me the way to his house?" asked Monsieur Givet.

"Why, yes," replied Marie, surprised. "It's straight up through the forest—but I shouldn't go up there if I were you, sir. The path will be bad after all this snow."

"I have business with him," replied Monsieur Givet briefly. "Perhaps you will point out the path to me from the door. On the way down I will come and say good-bye to Lucien."

Monsieur Givet thought he had never seen the forest more beautiful as he toiled up the track that late afternoon. The trees were bowed down and the cones frosted and starred. What must it be like, thought Monsieur Givet, to be this old man and live alone among all this silence and peace, sharing the secrets of the forest, and watching the coming and going of the unhurried seasons? He began to look forward to meeting him, and found his heart was beating faster than usual.

As he left the forest he could see the hut standing half-way up the meadow, with the snow piled high against its walls. The old man had dug a little path as far as the trees—almost as though he were expecting a visitor, thought Monsieur Givet, picking his way along it.

He knocked softly on the door and entered without waiting for a reply. The old man sat hunched up over his stove whittling wood and drawing at his pipe. The goat and the cat sat one each side of him for company, and Monsieur Givet took the chair the other side of the stove.

"Well," said the old man, still not looking up, "did you get there safely, Lucien?"

"It's not Lucien," replied Monsieur Givet softly, and the old man jumped and looked up. And then they sat staring at each other as though they had each seen a ghost—and yet uncertainly, as though the ghost might possibly be true after all.

"I have come to give you back this money," said Monsieur Givet at last. "I don't want money to help that child. In the circumstances I will do it free, if it can be done."

"Then the boy broke his promise," growled the old man, and he leaned his chin on his stick and stared and stared and stared.

"He did not break his promise," replied Monsieur Givet. "He told me nothing but that it was given him by an old man, and that it was the payment of a debt. But I do not accept large sums of money from peasant boys without making sure that they were come by honestly. I had no difficulty in finding from other people who you were, and where you lived."

There was another long, long silence. "Is that all you came to say?" said the old man at last—and his voice sounded old and weary and hopeless.

Monsieur Givet got up quickly and knelt down beside the bowed figure of the old man.

"Need we pretend any more?" he said. "Surely we are both quite sure of each other! I've come to take you home, Father, and to tell you how much we've missed you and wanted you."

Chapter Twenty-one

It was on a clear spring morning, just over a year from the time when Dani had fallen, that a group of people gathered at the railway station amid the unbelievably green fields starred with flowers.

To Lucien, the months had tended to drag by, with Annette so far away in the doctor's house, and Dani gaily amusing the other children in the hospital. But now things were different at school. He had shown how sorry he was by his perilous journey across the mountain and so was accepted once more. He also knew that the Saviour was breaking down his hardness and changing him into a kind and loving person.

His old friend of the mountain, the wood-carver, had gone to live with his son Monsieur Givet. Lucien missed him, but had become fast friends with Grandmother, sharing her delight at Annette's postcards and Dani's pictures—" Me in bed ",—" Me out of bed ",—" Me and Annette ", and others.

Today, the great day, the day when Annette would return with Dani, he was nervous, half wishing he hadn't come. But he needn't have worried. The train suddenly roared in, and there were Annette and Dani at the window clamouring to be let out.

Dani gave one glance at the group of well-loved faces all pressed so close to welcome him, and in that glance he noticed Lucien standing apart, and for an instant wondered why. His loving, happy little heart wanted to gather them all together about him, and he tumbled out of the train, broke through the crowd, and ran straight to Lucien.

"Look, Lucien," he shouted, "I can walk! Your doctor you found made me better, and I can run just as though I never fell into the stream. Look, Grandmother! look, Daddy! I'm running without my crutch! and look, Klaus, here's your kitten. Isn't he big, Grandmother? nearly as big as Klaus!"

Klaus and the kitten simply hated each other, and snarled and scratched and swore dreadfully. Dani and Grandmother struggled to keep them apart, the crowd laughed, the train rattled off, and Annette clung to her father as though she would never let go of him again.

Only Lucien had turned away, because he found there were tears in his eyes. He had been honoured above everybody—his sin was forgiven and forgotten for ever—Dani could walk just as though he had never fallen.

And as he turned he noticed that the almond tree on the platform had burst into flower at the top. Yesterday there was nothing but bare branches; but spring had proved too strong for it, and straight from the naked wood had crowded the starry pink blossoms.

The winter was over and gone, the flowers had appeared on the earth—the time of the singing of birds had come.

THE END